"I'm asking you to come with me."

As he spoke, Leo swung around to face her.

"Why?" Gael asked derisively. "So that the whole club can see what a devoted husband you are?"

"I want you to come as my wife," Leo said grimly.

"Your wife!" Gael laughed mirthlessly. "I'm just the poor fool who fell for your all-too-obvious charms. The dupe you're using to take your vengeance out on and to further your career. All right, I'll go because that's part of our bargain, but let's not have any false ideas about it. I go on sufferance."

He took his hands from his pockets, and she saw they were clenched tightly. "It doesn't have to be that way, Gael."

She stared at him, trying to read his expression. "Yes, it does," she said heavily. "There'll never be any other way."

Other titles by

SALLY
WENTWORTH
IN HARLEQUIN PRESENTS

Other titles by

SALLY
WENTWORTH
IN HARLEQUIN ROMANCES

SALLY
WENTWORTH

betrayal in bali

Harlequin Books

TORONTO • LONDON • LOS ANGELES • AMSTERDAM
SYDNEY • HAMBURG • PARIS • STOCKHOLM • ATHENS • TOKYO

Harlequin Presents edition published November 1980
ISBN 0-373-10396-4

Original hardcover edition published in 1980
by Mills & Boon Limited

CHAPTER ONE

'IT'S all right, Clive, really. I can quite easily get home by train.'

'Nonsense! I wouldn't dream of letting my favourite sister-in-law go home alone this late at night. It won't take me a minute to get the car out.'

'Okay, if you insist. Thanks.' Gael turned to say goodbye to her sister as Clive shrugged himself into his sheepskin car-coat. 'Thanks again for a super meal, Velma—and say goodbye to the children for me.'

The older girl gave her a hug and a kiss. 'I will. They absolutely loved the presents you brought them, but you really shouldn't be so generous, you know. You'll spoil them.'

Gael laughed. 'Who else have I got to spoil?' She went outside and turned back to wave. 'Goodnight, Velma.'

She shivered as she got in the car; there was a sharp nip of cold in the air even though it was March, and Clive had to clear the windscreen of a thin layer of frost before they could start away.

'Soon get warm once we get going,' he told her as he bent to switch on the heater.

Gael leaned back in her seat, feeling pleasantly full and sleepy. Velma was a good cook and she had enjoyed the celebration dinner to mark Clive's new job as senior sales representative for a worldwide organisation. He was still talking about it as they drove along, the wine and drinks they had consumed during the course of the evening making him even more loquacious than usual, whereas it just made Gael feel sleepy. So she hardly listened as he went on about it being the opportunity of a lifetime, how he would be able to afford a better house and send the kids to really good schools now. She liked her brother-in-law very much and was genuinely pleased that he was doing well, but she had heard it all already that evening. She leant her head back on the head-rest and gradually began to nod off.

Her first indication of danger came when she was thrown violently sideways, only her safety belt saving her from hitting her head against the side window. To her horror she saw that they were in a violent skid, the car corkscrewing across the empty road as Clive sought vainly to control the vehicle.

'Hold on!' he yelled at her. 'We've hit a patch of ice!' He tried to turn into the skid, but the ice must have been wet because they careered further across the road, just as another car, its headlights blazing, came fast round the bend towards them.

'Oh, my God! Look out!' Clive yanked at the wheel and this time the tires gripped, sending the car spinning round, but too late to avert a collision as the oncoming car smashed into the back of them.

The noise was terrible—the immense thud of impact, a great grinding and shrieking of metal, the roar of an engine close behind her head. But worst of all a terrified scream that went on and on. And it wasn't until every other noise had died away that she realised the voice was her own.

'Gael! Gael, stop it!' Clive gripped her shoulders hard and shook her a little. 'Are you hurt?'

Her screams died abruptly and she stared at him, trying

to gather her shattered senses. 'I—I don't know.' She clutched at his sleeves helplessly.

'Look, we've got to get out,' he said urgently. 'Can you open your door?'

'N-no. It's all buckled.'

'Then you'll have to get out my side, my door's okay.' He heaved it open and almost fell out on to the road, then reached in to help her out. Immediately the air struck cold, so cold. Clive put his arm round her and led her across the verge to a low stone wall.

'Here, sit here while I go and check on the other car.'

Gael sat down obediently, but as he moved away she saw the cars, Clive's with the front part more or less intact, but the other car, what had once been a white Jaguar sports car but was now virtually unrecognisable, was almost completely embedded in the rear of Clive's estate car, its still hot engine only inches away from the passenger head-rest. As she realised the closeness of her escape, Gael began to tremble violently, her whole body shaking convulsively.

Clive seemed to be gone a long time, but then she heard his footsteps, loud on the tarmac road, coming slowly towards her. Pulling her coat tighter around her, Gael looked up at him expectantly. He stared down at her, his face, even in the light of the sodium lamps, completely drained of colour. She thought inconsequentially that he suddenly seemed much older.

Slowly, as if he found it difficult to speak, he said, 'There's a man and a girl. They're—they're both—dead.'

Gael stared at him, for a moment too stunned to speak, but then her mind rejected such terrible news and she said chokingly, 'But they can't be! You—you must have made a mistake. They must be alive.'

She jumped up suddenly and began to run towards the cars. Clive reached out a hand to stop her, but she shook him off and ran behind the tangled mess of metal.

'No, Gael, don't look!'

But it was too late, she had already seen the body of the girl, half inside the car, half lying in the frost-rimed road. She was young, about twenty-five or so, and beautiful, with lovely features and long-lashed eyes, her dark hair flowing silky smooth to her white dress. Only the dress wasn't white any more, it was deeply stained with blood, and the lovely eyes stared blindly up at the night sky.

Clive took Gael's arm and led her away, but she was hardly aware of it.

He sat her on the wall again and spoke urgently. 'I've got to go and get help. Will you be all right here, Gael?'

Somehow she nodded and managed, 'Yes. Yes, I'm all right. You go.'

He looked at her uncertainly for a moment, then took off his coat and wrapped it round her before hurrying away.

His footsteps died away and she was left alone with the tangled wreckage. It was very quiet and dark, no houses nearby to light the blackness beyond the glow of the street lamps, no other cars out on the road so late on this cold, freezing night. She was completely alone except for ... except for ... The memory of what she had seen filled her mind, nausea rose in her chest until she turned and was horribly sick over the wall, tears pouring down her face and her body jerking spasmodically as shock hit her.

It seemed a terribly long time before she heard someone running towards her and looked up eagerly to see Clive emerge out of the darkness, his panting breaths turning immediately to little clouds of steam in the cold night air.

'I found a public telephone,' he told her as he slumped beside her on the wall. 'The police and ambulance should be here any minute.'

He put an arm round her and she was overwhelmingly grateful for his warmth and strength, and glad that it would soon be all over so that she could be safe at home in her own small flat.

But after a moment Clive said awkwardly, 'Gael, I've been thinking—when the police come they're bound to make me take a breathalyser test. It's standard practice whenever there's been an accident. And—well, quite frankly I don't think I'd pass. We had quite a few drinks tonight one way and another.'

Gael looked up in surprise at his anxious face. 'But the crash wasn't your fault—you said we hit a patch of ice.'

'So we did. But the fact still remains that the police would consider me unfit to drive. And if they did prosecute me for drunken driving—well, can't you see what that would mean, Gael? I'd probably lose my licence, and if I lost that then I'd definitely lose this new job. Even if I only got an endorsement the company might still think twice about employing someone who drank too much.' His voice became very bitter. 'And there goes the new house and everything we wanted for the kids, just as we had it all within our grasp, too. It isn't fair, damn it, it just isn't fair!'

He got up and moved moodily away from her. Gael looked at him in distress, deeply upset that his life should be shattered in this way. Gropingly she tried to comfort him. 'But it may not be as bad as you think. I'm a witness, I can tell them that you skidded on the ice.'

'It won't make any difference, they'll just look at the result of the breathalyser and I'll get blamed for the whole terrible mess. Your testimony won't mean a thing.' He stared down at her morosely, but then his expression changed suddenly, became almost eager. 'But if you really want to help ...'

'Yes, of course I do,' Gael assured him. 'Have you thought of something?'

'Well, it's an idea.' He came to sit beside her again and looked at her speculatively. 'And it's a lot to ask—but I know how fond you are of Velma and the kids.'

'What? What is it?' Gael asked impatiently.

'Well——' for a moment he looked discomfited, then went on, 'the thought occurred to me that if you said that you were driving ...'

Gael stared at him uncomprehendingly. 'Me? But I wasn't. It wouldn't be true!'

Clive caught hold of her hands. 'But only we know that. And what have you got to lose, Gael? You don't even own a car yet. But I've got everything to lose, everything Velma and I have been working and striving for all these years. Lost in a matter of seconds.'

In the distance they heard the whine of a police siren and his voice became urgent, entreating. 'Please, Gael, say you'll do it. It means so much to us!'

Gael gazed into his face, realising that the man she had looked on as a brother, who she had thought to be strong and upright, was just as weak and human as everyone else. She turned her head away, unable to bear the look of fear in his eyes.

'All right,' she agreed woodenly.

'Thank God! Gael, you'll never know how grateful I am! And Velma will be too.'

But she couldn't listen to his exuberant thanks and

moved quickly away to lean against the lamp-post as the police car came in sight and drew up beside them.

The next few hours went by in a sort of numb waking nightmare. As Clive had predicted, the police made her take a breathalyser test as soon as Clive told them she had been driving, and as she had drunk as much as he had, the alcohol content was over the limit. Clive explained about the patch of ice, insisted on taking a policeman to see it, and she supposed they weren't too hard on her, but their faces became very grim when they saw the bodies in the other car and thereafter they treated her with an icy politeness that bordered closely on contempt and made her feel absolutely wretched.

They were taken to the nearest police station where they were made to sign written statements and then had to sit while arrangements were made about the car. There seemed to be a lot of waiting around, during which time they sat on a bench in the lobby. At one point Clive went to take her hand and squeeze it reassuringly, but Gael immediately disengaged herself and put her hand in her pocket, her set face turned away.

While they waited the belongings of the two crash victims were brought in and squad cars sent off to inform their next of kin. The realisation that their relatives would blame her for the deaths made Gael cringe inside and the room began to sway so that she had to grip hard to the bench to stop herself from fainting.

A reporter from the local paper phoned in, but the police wouldn't give any details, and after he'd put the phone down she heard the duty sergeant say to a colleague, 'We'll have to keep this one hush-hush; seems the man in the car was married and was out on the sly with a girl-friend. His wife thought he was in London for a conference.'

But shortly after that they were allowed to go and Gael was driven the rest of the way to her flat in a northern suburb of London in a police car, while Clive was taken back to his own home. He tried to take her aside and talk to her before they left, but she just told him that she was too tired and walked away from him. The flat was a haven, a sanctuary, and she couldn't wait to get inside and shut the front door, leaning against it for a few minutes until her palpitating nerves had calmed a little. Then she made herself some soup and sat huddled over the glowing bars of the electric fire until she was so tired that she just had to go to bed.

The following week she and Clive had to go and give evidence at the inquests on the victims, but there were two separate hearings, first the man and then the woman, the former in the morning and the second one later in the afternoon. At the first inquest there was a woman dressed entirely in black who looked at Gael as if she was a murderer. She had, as the man's wife, to give evidence of identification, and soon broke into heartbroken sobs until she was led away by other relatives. During the whole proceedings no mention was made of the girl being in the car with him. Later, the girl was identified by her uncle as Julia Symons. It seemed that her parents were too overcome by grief to be present; she was their only child.

At the court case Gael was found to be partly responsible for the accident, had her driving licence taken away for two years and was severely reprimanded by the magistrate, although Clive also came in for some censure for allowing her, a newly qualified driver, to drive his car in icy conditions when she had been drinking. Which last gave her a

modicum of satisfaction even if it didn't lessen the knowledge that she had lost not only her licence but her good
name.

As the next few weeks passed and spring took the chill
out of the weather and began to awaken the trees and
flowers in the parks, Gael contented herself with phoning
her sister, only going down to visit when Clive had started
his new job and was away on a training course. Gradually
the hurt and disappointment he had inflicted became less
deep, and she came to realise that perhaps the lie had been
for the best; Velma was so very happy, but nothing seemed
to dim the ever-recurring nightmare in which she saw the
girl's body lying in the roadway, her hair mingling with the
blood on her white dress. It was then she would wake suddenly, hot and shaking with fear, to lie awake for a long
time staring into the darkness, too scared to go back to
sleep.

But at least the horror only came back at night; during
the day she could keep herself busy at work and try to tire
herself so that she was too exhausted to dream. Gael considered herself extremely lucky in that she had been
selected straight from art school to be an assistant at the
Capel Gallery, one of the leading private art galleries in the
West End of London. Here she was able to indulge her love
of paintings to the utmost as she learnt how to hang the
pictures to the best advantage for light and colour and was
initiated into the arts of restoration and cleaning, watching
what had been dark, almost featureless paintings come alive
under her careful hands.

Her years at art college had been some of the happiest in
her life and she had been one of the most promising
students, being equally successful in both oils and water-

colours. She hoped that eventually, some time in the dim and distant future, she would be able to develop her own style sufficiently to earn a living by her painting, but she knew that she still had a lot to learn and was more than happy to have the opportunity to study the work of other artists while painting as much as she could in her spare time.

At present most of her time in the gallery was spent in the Watercolour and Print Rooms, but from twelve until one every day she took over from a senior assistant and manned the desk by the main entrance while he went to lunch. This always gave her a pleasant thrill of responsibility as she placed her nameplate on the desk and prepared to deal with the queries of potential customers, interview hopeful artists who brought in new pictures, and even occasionally sell a painting. This hour could sometimes be one of their busiest, especially if they were mounting an exhibition of a particular artist, because then people would wander in during their lunch breaks, and if the weather was wet or cold and people wanted to while the time away in the warm, then the numbers increased considerably, although very few of them had any intention of buying.

It was on a day such as this, when it was teeming with rain outside and she had been pestered by questions about various paintings, that her patience wore a little thin, and when she was asked yet again for information she answered shortly, without looking up from where she was writing out a receipt, 'All the information you want is contained in the catalogue. They're on the table by the entrance.'

Dryly the questioner replied, 'Unfortunately there don't seem to be any there.'

Gael glanced across at the table and saw that it was

empty. 'Oh, I'm so sorry, I'll get some more.' She swivelled round in her chair and took a fresh pile of catalogues from the cupboard behind her and then rose to give one to the customer. She found herself offering it to a very tall, dark-haired man in his early thirties, but what struck her most forcibly about him wasn't his height but his deep tan, a sharp contrast to the pallid, winter faces all around him. He was so brown in fact that for a brief second Gael thought that the colour might be natural, but the impression was immediately dispelled; there was no mistaking his evenly-featured good looks and the grey eyes that were regarding her intently as anything other than European.

'Thank you,' his eyes went down to her nameplate. 'Miss Gael Markham,' he added as he took the catalogue from her.

He went away as she hurried to put the rest of the catalogues on the table and she didn't see him again until just before one when he came up to the desk and said that he would like to buy a picture.

'It's number thirty-five,' he told her.

Gael flipped the pages of the catalogue and found that number thirty-five was a spring landscape and one of her favourites. 'Oh, that's one of his best,' she exclaimed.

The man's left eyebrow rose rather quizzically. 'You know about paintings? You're not just a receptionist?'

She flushed slightly. 'I studied art for four years. I know a little, but I'm certainly not an expert.'

'Then perhaps you know enough to give me some guidance about another couple of paintings that I like the look of.' And to Gael's surprise the man put a firm hand under her elbow and led her into the Watercolour Room.

Once there, he pointed out two paintings, one a view of

boats being repaired in a boatyard, the other of a woman sitting in the doorway of a crofter's cottage, knitting.

'I want a present for some elderly friends of mine,' he informed her. 'I think the subject matter in either of these would be suitable, but I want to give the one that is most likely to appreciate in value. Now, which do you think?' The grey eyes, pale in his tanned face, turned to look down at her expectantly.

Gael found herself held for a moment by his eyes, but then turned to look at the two paintings. She couldn't be sure, it had been too faint, but she certainly thought that there had been a hint of challenge in his eyes and voice, as if he didn't really believe that a girl could give him the information he wanted. But she hadn't wasted her time at the gallery, and with only a few moment's thought, she answered, 'If I wanted to buy one of these pictures purely as an investment then I would definitely choose the woman in the cottage.'

'Will you tell me why?'

'Because the boatyard picture was painted by a fairly young artist who hasn't yet developed his style, and that one is an imitation of the style of a better-known artist. Also, because he's young he's going to paint hundreds more pictures before he's through and it will take a long time for his early works to appreciate in value while he is still painting and improving his technique. And the subject, although pleasant, is quite common; lots of male artists like painting boats.' She pointed to the other picture. 'Whereas this one was painted by a Scottish artist, a man who retired to the Hebrides and only took up painting very late in life, so he has few pictures in circulation and his subject is quite unusual. Therefore it's a much better short-term investment.'

She had been so engrossed in her little lecture that she had almost forgotten her listener, but now she turned to find him watching her with a strangely cold, intent look in his eyes, but this changed and he smiled down at her, his face immediately becoming completely different, warm and faintly admiring.

'Well, well, so you really do know your stuff. All right, on your recommendation I'll buy the Hebridian one as well.'

They walked back to her desk and she filled in the sales forms. His name, she learnt, was Leo Kane and he gave his address as the Army & Navy Club, one of the most exclusive clubs in London. By the time she had arranged for the pictures to be delivered to him the senior assistant had returned from lunch, so Gael left the final arrangements of the sale to him and hurried away to fetch her mac and umbrella, her tummy already starting to make hungry noises.

The rain was still teeming down and Gael paused at the entrance as she put up her umbrella, grimacing at the rotten weather; it seemed as if it hadn't stopped raining for weeks and that the spring would never come. She started to hurry down the steps, intending to head towards the nearest hamburger bar, when a voice she recognised said, 'You couldn't possibly share that thing, could you?' and she turned to see her recent customer sheltering in a nearby doorway.

She hesitated, taken aback, but before she could speak he seemed to take her agreement for granted and crossed to her side, ducking under the shelter of the umbrella.

'I've been trying to get a taxi, but I think there must be some black hole that they all disappear into whenever it rains,' he told her as he began to walk along, Gael perforce falling into step beside him.

'Where are you going?' she asked rather stiffly, none too pleased at his high-handed treatment.

He took the umbrella from where she had been reaching up to hold it over his head. 'You'd better give me that—these things are positive eye-gougers.' He looked at her and gave a slightly crooked smile which robbed his remark of malice. 'I'm taking you out to lunch, of course.'

Gael gave a little gasp of surprise. 'Just because we're sharing an umbrella it doesn't mean that...'

He shook his head. 'I owe you lunch for your advice about the paintings. I'm really very grateful.'

'It was nothing. I was glad to be able to help. You really don't owe me anything, Mr Kane. And anyway, I only have an hour for lunch, so there's really no point in...'

But again she wasn't allowed to finish. He suddenly said, 'Good God, there's a cab!' and stepped towards the curb, his arm raised authoritatively.

Wonder of wonders it came, and Gael looked at him in respect. Anybody who could stop a London taxi in a rainstorm had to be quite something. She went to back away and hurry on, but he caught hold of her arm and almost propelled her into it.

'Now just a minute!' Gael exclaimed in annoyance. 'If this is your idea of some kind of pick-up, then you've chosen the wrong girl!'

He turned to her, and somehow he seemed much bigger and broader in the confines of the musty, damp-smelling taxi. Raising an eyebrow quizzically, he sat back and pulled a packet of cigarettes from his pocket, offering her one, his mouth twisting with amusement.

'Good heavens, is that what you think? That I'm trying to pick you up? I assure you I had every intention of coming back into the gallery as soon as I'd found a taxi and formally asking you to have lunch with me as a token of my appreciation. And strange as it may seem to you, I'm not in the habit of making casual pick-ups. I haven't quite had to resort to that yet.'

There was a note of sarcasm in his voice that put Gael on the defensive. 'I beg your pardon,' she said stiffly, and then thought: No, I bet you don't. You're much too sure of yourself for that. And too good-looking.

She accepted a cigarette, her eyes automatically looking to see if he was wearing a wedding ring when he held a lighter for her. His hands were strong and slim—and completely ringless. Sitting back in the seat, she said, 'It's very kind of you to offer to take me to lunch, Mr Kane, but I do really only have an hour.'

'Don't worry, we'll be there in five minutes.'

The taxi drove down Regent Street, threaded its way through the congestion of Piccadilly Circus where Eros stood on his pedestal, the rain having swept the steps below the statue clean of the usual crowd of young tourists, down past Trafalgar Square with its black needle of Nelson's Column and into the Strand where it pulled up at the discreet entrance to the Savoy. Gael raised her eyebrows; Mr Leo Kane certainly did things in style!

Once inside, he helped her off with her mac and gave it, together with his military type trench-coat, to the cloakroom attendant, then led her towards the entrance to the Grill Room.

'I thought we'd go straight in instead of having a drink in the bar first, as you're restricted for time.'

'Yes, of course.' Gael looked at the plush surroundings, noting the expensive furs of the woman in front of them.

She gave a rather nervous laugh. 'I'm not really dressed for this kind of place, you know.'

His eyes ran over her tall, slim figure in the pale blue sweater and check skirt, a matching silk scarf knotted loosely round her neck, and on to her finely-boned face with the heavy-fall of fair hair curling on to her shoulders. 'You look fine,' he said appreciatively.

Gael flushed, annoyed with herself for having given him an excuse to look her over so openly, almost as if she had deliberately wanted him to do it. She sighed inwardly; you had to be so careful what you said to men, they were always on the look-out for any opening, however slight, to turn a relationship into a sexual one. During her years at art school, Gael had had many boy-friends and had soon come to the conclusion that all men had one-track minds, and if you wanted to keep them then they expected you to go along with them, refusing to take no for an answer and resorting to downright nastiness or moral blackmail if they didn't get what they wanted. Even the nicest ones got impatient when you refused to go the whole way, muttering about old-fashioned attitudes and giving her lectures on women being liberated and it was natural for them to need sex just as much as a man, that she had the right to sleep with anyone whenever she wanted to. Her usual retort to this was that if she was liberated like they said, then her body was her own and she had as much right *not* to give it if she didn't want to, and she didn't—definitely, after which remark very few persisted and went after easier game instead.

Soon after she came to London, however, she had met a suave and very handsome man who she had really thought might be the man she could marry, but had been bitterly

hurt when he had turned out to be just like the rest. Oh, his
approach had been far more subtle, his line far more
persuasive; and she had almost been on the point of sur-
rendering herself to him when she found out that he was
already married. And then he had had the nerve to say
What did it matter? They could still be together in the
evenings after work and before he went home to his wife!
So now Gael was off men completely, and had been for the
last few months. And liking the arrangement very much,
thank you! So she had no wish to get involved with Mr
Kane in any way whatsoever, she told herself firmly as the
head waiter led them towards their table, and repeated it
hastily when she moved to let a waiter go past and found
herself close to him, his hand warm on her arm, the subtle
aftershave and completely masculine smell of him filling
her nostrils.

He let her decide for herself what she wanted to eat, but
was quite definite about which wine they would have,
seeming to be quite knowledgeable on the subject. While
he ordered, Gael had more opportunity to study him and
decided she rather liked his air of authority, the decisive
way he spoke, his voice rather deep but well-modulated
and accentless. She tried to guess at his background and
thought he probably came from the south of England with
a public school and Oxford education.

He turned back to her and she immediately assumed an
interest in her surroundings.

'Have you been here before?' he asked.

Gael smiled and shook her head. 'No, it's quite beyond
the means of humble art gallery assistants.'

'Have you worked there long?'

'Nearly nine months.'

'And I think you said you studied art before that, didn't you?'

His manner was very easy and gradually he drew her out, getting her to tell him about herself, her work and her background, until they were interrupted by the waiter bringing their first course.

Gael took advantage of the lull to ask, 'Do you live in England?'

He grinned. 'Which is a polite way of asking where have I been to get as brown as a Red Indian!' He paused as he broke up a roll, then said, 'I don't have any permanent home. I was born and brought up in Kent, but now I travel all over the world, wherever my company cares to send me. For the past year I've been in South America, but at the moment I have a three months' leave in between assignments. I'm not sure yet where I shall be sent to next. Could be anywhere,' he told her cheerfully.

'How marvellous,' Gael exclaimed. 'I'd love to be able to travel. You must have seen some fascinating places?'

'Quite a few.' He didn't enlarge on the point, however, but asked her instead about her family.

'My parents died quite some time ago,' she told him. 'But I have a sister who lives not too far away, although my brother-in-law hopes to buy a new house soon.'

'Your brother-in-law? Ah, yes.' He said it almost absent-mindedly, and for a moment she wondered if she was boring him, but he said, 'And you have no other relations?'

'No one close, no.' She gave a little frown. 'How about you?'

'Oh, I'm an orphan too. And any relations I have I've lost touch with; the closest emigrated to Australia years ago—

and that's one country I've never been sent to, so there's been no reason to make contact again.'

This seemed rather a lonely kind of existence, so Gael said reassuringly, 'But you have lots of friends—the ones you bought the painting for, for instance?'

'Oh, yes.' For a moment he became very still, a mask descending over his face, but the mood was quickly gone as he blinked and leant forward to pour some more wine into her glass.

'Are you spending the whole of your leave in London, Mr Kane?' Gael asked to fill the sudden break in the conversation.

'I haven't made any definite plans, although I do have a tentative arrangement to spend two or three weeks with some friends who have a villa in Ibiza. It depends how things work out.' His rather heavy-lidded, long-lashed eyes settled on her. 'And the name's Leo, if you remember?' he added enigmatically.

He switched the conversation then to less personal subjects, displaying a wide knowledge, sure of his viewpoints and not afraid to state them, which he did eloquently but holding himself well in hand, never letting himself get carried away by his opinions. But the conversation was by no means a monologue; he made a point of asking her views as well and seemed genuinely interested in what she had to say, so that Gael became animated, her eyes, a deep cornflower-blue, lighting up with enthusiasm and often with appreciative amusement as she laughed at some dry witticism he made.

She had never had a date with anyone as old as Leo before, all her boy-friends had been nearer her own age of twenty-two, and they suddenly seemed extremely immature in comparison; even the last one, who had turned out to be married, had only been about twenty-six. And Gael couldn't help but enjoy the experience of being treated like an equal, as a person whose views and opinions mattered. The implied compliment was far headier than any fulsome flattery. She found that she was beginning to like Mr Leo Kane, of almost anywhere in the world, rather a lot and she put herself out to amuse him, not only to be an interesting companion, but because she liked the way he threw back his head when he laughed, his eyes crinkling up at the corners. But most of all it was some animal sort of magnetism in him that attracted her, as if his languid, almost lazy manner hid an inner strength that was like a coiled spring, hidden except for an odd moment when it had shown in a sudden alertness in his eyes, or his hand tightening on his glass. She had an overwhelming feeling that he would be the right man to have around if you were ever in trouble, that he would be able to deal with any situation, however nasty. And certainly not the type to let anyone else take the blame for something that he had done, she thought rather bleakly as her mind went back to the car crash, her body shivering involuntarily at the memory.

Perhaps a shadow crossed her face, because Leo put out his hand to cover hers—the first time he had touched her, except impersonally.

'Is something the matter?' he asked, looking at her closely.

Gael gave a little shrug and shook off the mood. 'No, it's nothing.'

'Just someone walking over your grave?' he said lightly.

The hand under his trembled violently. 'That's a stupid saying!' she exclaimed sharply.

For a second the cold alertness was back in his eyes and she felt his hand tighten, but then he relaxed and said smoothly, 'Of course it is. I'm sorry. Let's have a liqueur, shall we? Have you ever had a Baileys? I think you'll like it.'

He called the waiter and Gael found that she did indeed like the richly smooth whisky and cream drink, sipping it appreciatively as he told her an anecdote about an encounter with an angry rhinoceros when he had been working in Africa some years ago and had gone with several of the men in his company on a week's safari into a game park.

'We all scattered in different directions and ran like hell, just hoping and praying that the animal would choose someone else to chase, but all the time we could hear these great charging footsteps coming behind us and terribly heavy, panting breathing almost down our necks, and we were convinced the brute would get us any second.'

'You mean there was more than one rhino?' Gael asked wonderingly.

He grinned. 'No, the rhino had turned and gone back to its mate as soon as we scattered, but the land we were running across was a strange kind of mud flat and the footsteps and breathing were only echoes of the noise we were making ourselves, but all of us were so darn scared we didn't even stop to look round and we ran until we just couldn't run any further. And all the time the native drivers in the safari cars were falling about the place with laughter!'

The anecdote was funny in itself, but it also told Gael that Leo didn't take himself too seriously, that he was capable of laughing at himself, and she found that she rather liked that. In fact there were a great many qualities about Leo Kane that she rather liked. Hey, steady there, my girl, she told herself sternly. He's only here on leave, remember? In a few weeks he'll be away to some distant and exotic land without a passing thought for the girl he dated. Not that he's likely to want to see me again. He's probably got a little black book bulging with telephone numbers, and he's so good-looking and so downright macho that they would all drop everything and fall over themselves to go out with him. Not that she cared, of course, because she had given up men and so wasn't interested. But she had enjoyed today and couldn't help but wonder if he *would* ask her for another date. Of course she would say no, but it would be interesting to find out whether she had made a favourable impression and he wanted to take it further, although he might only have asked her to lunch because he didn't want to eat alone and it would while away an hour or two.

The thought of time made her come back to the basic reality of work and she gave a gasp of horror as she looked at her watch. 'Oh, no! It's nearly two-thirty!'

There was a rush then to pay the bill and find a cab. But the rain had stopped at last and there was even a weak sun trying to push its way through the clouds, so now that no one wanted one there were taxis in plenty and they were soon pulling up outside the gallery.

Leo helped her out and turned to pay the driver. Gael waited to thank him; he hadn't said anything about seeing her again and she was more than a little piqued, although she told herself she was glad, she certainly didn't want to get involved.

As he turned she held out her hand and said politely, 'Thank you for a lovely lunch. It was very kind of you. Goodbye.'

He took her hand and shook it. 'And thank you for your advice. Goodbye.'

Gael hesitated for just a fraction longer, then nodded and turned to go into the gallery.

She had reached the second step when Leo said, 'Gael,' and she turned to look back at him. He grinned. 'Tomorrow?'

Her face lit up with a radiant smile. 'I'd like that!'

CHAPTER TWO

THE weak rays of sun that had struggled through the clouds on that first day quickly developed into a beautiful springtime, transforming London from drab, grey streets of concrete into bright, golden-pavemented avenues as window-boxes brimmed with daffodils and the trees in the many parks burst into brilliant leaf. And Gael's attraction to Leo grew just as rapidly, seeming to become deeper every time she saw him. If he had had a little black book he appeared to have thrown it away, because they saw each other almost every day, driving out into the country or to the coast at the weekends, and going to the theatre or ballet during the week. He didn't seem to care much for the high-life and never took her to a night-club where they could dance, which was rather a disappointment, but sometimes—the times Gael liked best of all—they would dine together in some small, exclusive restaurant where the lighting was dim and the service unobtrusive and they would talk or sit in companionable silence, and sometimes Leo would turn to her and smile and cover her hand with his so that her heart filled with a wonderful kind of contentment that was at the same time alive with excitement and anticipation.

Whether Leo had the same feelings for her Gael wasn't certain, for, although he paid her compliments that did wonders for her morale, he said nothing about how he felt towards her. And for a while, in the early stages, that didn't seem to matter, it was only when she caught herself dreaming about what it would be like to be married to him that how Leo felt about her suddenly became terribly important. She tried then to draw back, telling herself that he wasn't the type to settle down, that in a few weeks his leave would end and she would never see him again. Oh, perhaps he would promise to write, might even do so a couple of times, but then he would forget her except to look back on with occasional nostalgia, or talk about over a drink with the boys, as the girl he'd had a good time with on his last leave in England. But it was no good; on the day she tried to be strong and said no, she was busy; to his invitation to dinner, he turned up at her flat almost hidden behind a great armful of yellow roses and she didn't have the courage to turn him away.

And it was that night that he kissed her properly for the first time. Before, when he had greeted her or said goodnight, he had always given her a light kiss on the forehead, or touched his finger to his lips and then to hers. At first she had just been grateful that he hadn't made a pass which she would have had to turn down, but this had gradually changed to wondering why he didn't make a pass—and whether she now cared for him so much that she wouldn't be able to resist. But she wasn't even given the opportunity to find out; Leo seemed to want nothing more from her than her companionship, although it was obvious from the way he looked at her that he appreciated the way she dressed and looked. Inevitably she had become intrigued by his attitude and had tried to find out if he had had a woman in South America; he certainly didn't seem frustrated by his eighteen months in the wilds of Bolivia, where he had been involved with the building of a massive power plant, so presumably he had. But he didn't give anything away, just gave an amused smile as if he straight-away saw where her devious questions were heading and changed the subject.

So it came as something of a shock when he sat down on the sofa in her tiny flat, then caught her wrist and pulled her down on to his lap. His hand went to her neck, his thumb gently caressing her throat as his eyes searched her face. Then he drew her unresistingly towards him as his lips sought hers, gentle, exploring, but with an underlying hardness that sent a hot wave of sensuality and desire through her veins. Gael's arms went round his neck as she clung to him, all thoughts, all emotions lost in the wonder of his embrace. She had been kissed many times before, but it had never been like this—never, never like this! She pressed herself close to him, her lips opening under his, then saying his name over and over on a note of wonderment as he released her mouth to explore her neck, the hollows of her cheeks, her eyes. She knew that she ought to stop him before things went too far, but her whole body felt as if it was on fire, as if only his kisses could assuage it, and she turned her head to find his lips again, to kiss him with a passionate abandon that he didn't expect.

For a brief moment Leo returned the kiss with a fierce hunger, his hand tightening on her neck, but then he made a convulsive movement, his hands going to her shoulders as he forcefully pushed her away from him. Gael opened her eyes rather dazedly and found that he was staring at her, his breathing uneven, his fingers digging hard into her shoulders.

Abruptly he let her go and turned so that he slid his legs from under hers. 'I'm sorry,' he said, his voice uneven. 'I hadn't intended to take advantage of being alone with you here.' He stood up and turned away from her. 'May I have a drink?'

Without waiting for an answer he crossed to help himself, while slowly, her hands trembling, Gael straightened her clothes. She didn't know quite what had happened, she only knew that she hadn't wanted him to stop, she had wanted him to go on touching her, kissing her, to lose herself completely in the world of desire he had awakened in her.

Leo poured her a drink too, and handed it to her silently before going to sit in the armchair, looking rather broodingly down at his glass, swirling the liquid in it but not attempting to drink. He seemed lost in thought, far away from their intimate nearness of only a few moments ago. To regain that now was impossible, but she could at least have his attention. Reaching out, she put a hand on his knee and said tentatively, 'Leo?'

He didn't jump or anything, just raised his eyes and looked at her expressionlessly, but somehow he seemed hard and cold, almost resentful of her, so that she quickly drew back. Immediately the coldness left his face and he smiled and reached out to cover her hand.

'Sorry, I was miles away.' He leant back easily in his chair and played with her fingers. 'What would you like to do this weekend? How about if we drive to the Blackwater Estuary and hire a boat?'

'For the whole weekend?' Gael asked rather unsteadily.

His mouth twisted into an ironical smile. 'I rather think that after tonight that might be a little unwise, don't you?'

Slowly she said, 'I don't know. Would it?' and waited with fast-beating heart for his answer.

Leo let go of her hand and put a long finger under her chin, tilting her head to look at him. 'Oh, yes, I think so,' he replied steadily. Then added deliberately, 'Little one.'

So that was it; he thought her too young—or himself too old for her. Probably had moral scruples about making love to anyone more than ten years younger than himself, or something equally stupid, Gael thought in a sudden flash of anger. But the right to say no should be hers not his. Not that she had wanted to say no, her body had cried yes and yes and yes!

Sharply she said, 'I am of age, you know, Leo. I'm twenty-two, and well able to take care of myself. I've lived alone ever since I was eighteen and I'm completely in control of my own life.'

The cold look seemed to come down like a shutter over his face again and he looked directly at her as he said slowly, 'So you consider yourself responsible for your own actions, do you?'

Firmly she replied, 'Yes, I do.'

'And for the consequences?'

The question surprised her a little, but she answered readily enough, 'Yes, of course.'

For a minute longer he continued to regard her with that strange, brooding look, but then he seemed to pull himself together and abruptly changed the subject and was careful to keep their conversation on impersonal topics for the rest of the evening, and when he left he kissed her goodbye but gave her no encouragement to ask him to stay.

At the weekend they drove down to Malden and stayed overnight at a small country inn overlooking the estuary. But they stayed in separate rooms and Leo made no attempt to come to her, although Gael lay awake for hours, half afraid, half hoping, that he might.

He hired a sailing boat for the two days and tried to teach her to sail. Gael learnt quite quickly and would have enjoyed it if she hadn't been held in the grip of an intense feeling of frustration that made her quiver every time he accidentally touched her. On the Sunday she was tired and on edge, and although she tried to conceal her emotions, a tenseness grew between them that was impossible to ignore so that Leo cut short the day's sailing and headed for the shore.

Gael tried to pull herself together, told herself sternly that she was acting like a fool and a cheap one at that. Why, he had only kissed her properly once and here she was throwing herself at his head, almost begging him to take her to bed. But she had never felt like this before, never longed to feel a man's arms round her, or yearned for him to kiss and caress her. Angrily she dug her nails into her palms and tried to concentrate on sailing the boat, but it was no use; she just couldn't relax and give herself to the pleasure of just being with him any more. He had awakened emotions in her that she had never known before and nothing that she could do would ease their cruel torment.

They were both rather silent as they set out on the drive back to London, but at Chelmsford Leo stopped to fill up

with gas and said, 'I'm feeling a bit bushed. Will you drive
for a while, Gael?'

'Yes, of course.' She went to get out of the car and go
round to the driver's side, but then drew back. 'Oh, I
forgot. I'm sorry, I can't.'

Leo looked at her in some surprise. 'You mean you can't
drive?'

'Well, yes, I can. It's just that I'm not allowed to, I'm
afraid. You see, I had my licence taken away recently.'

Leo shut the door and put on his safety strap. 'Really?
What happened?' he asked as he pulled out of the garage.

'Oh, I was involved in an accident,' she told him reluctantly.

'A bad one? Were you hurt?'

'No.' Gael found that even now she couldn't talk about
it, that even thinking about it made the dreadful pictures
come back, so she said shortly, 'It was nothing.'

'Nothing? And yet you had your licence taken away?'

Angrily she snapped. 'I've already said so, haven't I?'
and turned to look fixedly out of the side window so that
he wouldn't ask her any more questions.

By the time they got back to her flat Gael was feeling
wretched about the dismal failure of the weekend, especially as she knew it was all her own fault. Leo carried her
case up for her and at her door she turned and said
hopefully, 'Would you like to come in for a drink?'

'Thanks, but I've got to take the car back to the hire
firm.' He hesitated, then said slowly, 'You remember I told
you some friends had invited me to stay with them in
Ibiza? Well, I've decided to fly out there tomorrow.'

Gael's hands tightened convulsively on her handbag and
it was long seconds before she said unsteadily, 'I—I see.

Will you—will you be coming back to England—afterwards?'

His voice, in contrast, was quite even as he answered, 'Yes, I expect so.'

Pride, everything was lost as she said desperately, 'Will I see you again?' But she couldn't look at him, couldn't bear to see her rejection in his face.

'Do you want to?'

Her eyes flew up then, her face naked and vulnerable, but she could read nothing from his, it was completely impersonal, gave her no clue to his feelings. But it wouldn't have mattered anyway, pride just didn't come into it any more. Huskily she said, 'Yes, I want to.'

'Then I'll give you a ring when I get back.' And, stepping forward, he kissed her briefly on the lips before turning and walking briskly away without a backward glance.

Gael leant against the wall and stared after him, her thoughts a chaotic mixture of surprise and hope. She had been so sure that he was going to end it, and yet he had left the way open for him to see her again. But such a tenuous opening! And so little to cling to! Just, I'll give you a ring when I get back. But he hadn't told her how long he would be away, when to expect his call. She tried feverishly to recall what he had said about Ibiza originally and seemed to remember that he had mentioned going for two or three weeks. So long! It seemed to stretch like light years. And in two or three weeks he could meet someone else, could have forgotten her completely. Slowly she turned and went into her flat, feeling more miserable than she had ever been in her life.

The days seemed to drag by even though Gael tried to keep herself busy by catching up on all the domestic chores that had been sadly neglected while she had been going out with Leo. But she found that she had no energy or enthusiasm for work either at home or in the gallery, often standing listlessly, just gazing abstractedly at nothing, which had twice earned her a rather exasperated rebuke from the senior assistant. Even trying to put her feelings on to canvas didn't work; every time she did so tears would ruin the picture as her mind filled with memories of Leo and she began to cry because she missed him so. Or else she became so enraged at her own stupidity that she angrily tore her efforts into shreds. Oh, damn! If this was what being in love was like, then she wished she'd never met the man. Because it was hell! hell! hell!

But mostly her mind was consumed by fear; fear that she would never see him again, that he wouldn't keep his promise and call her; fear that she had been too obvious and that he had realised she was falling for him and had quickly escaped from any possibility of a matrimonial trap. He was a man who loved to travel, who couldn't bear to be tied down by a wife, children, a mortgage. He must have been in the same situation a hundred times before and be adept at slipping out of the net. But he had said he would come back, she told herself a thousand times a day.

As the time passed she began staying in every evening in case he rang, and always hovered within earshot of the phone in the gallery, jumping nervously whenever it rang and rushing to be the first to answer it.

But gradually, as three weeks stretched into four, and the call never came, Gael began to lose hope. She lay awake at night, unable to sleep, and couldn't be bothered to cook proper meals, existing on junk food and things out of packets. Several times she had picked up the phone and started to dial the number of his club, but always her courage had failed her. Sternly she told herself that she was a liberated woman of the twentieth century, she had as much right to call a man and ask him for a date as he had to call her, but still she couldn't do it. What if he refused to take her call, what if he told her bluntly that he just wasn't interested? Anything was better than that.

Desperately she tried to pull herself together, especially at work, but her nerves and emotions were raw and vulnerable, the slightest reprimand from an impatient customer leaving her shaking and close to tears, so that she almost ran out of the gallery, to rush home just in case Leo rang, even though it was over a month now since he went away. And almost as if he had taken the sun with him, the weather had changed and the skies were like grey dishcloths every day, the rain filling the choked gutters and adding despondency to her unhappiness.

But one afternoon she came out of the gallery at the end of the day and he was there, wearing the familiar trenchcoat but the rain falling unheeded on his bare head. His tan, which had started to fade, was now as deep as ever again and it was almost like the first time as he stepped forward and said, 'Mind if I share your umbrella?'

Completely bereft of speech, Gael could only nod and let him take the umbrella from her suddenly slack hands. Putting an arm round her waist, Leo led her along but didn't attempt to speak, for which Gael was profoundly grateful; she was too full of choking happiness and relief to make any attempt at rational conversation right then.

They walked until they came to a square, one of those green oases that flower in the heart of London and are so beloved by the inhabitants, but Gael couldn't remember how they got there or which one it was. Leo led her to a comparatively dry bench under the spreading branches of a huge horse-chestnut tree, its growth of snow-white flowers like thousands of candles on a Christmas tree. They had the square to themselves, all the city workers hurrying to get home out of the rain, the noise of the rush-hour traffic muted by the trees and hedges. The only sounds were the occasional heavy droplets of rain from the tree and the noise of her own heart which was thudding so loudly that Gael was sure Leo must hear it.

Leo folded the umbrella and then turned to look at her. 'I missed you,' he said softly, and then bent to kiss her long and lingeringly.

Gael felt as if she had been dying of thirst and someone had offered her pure, clear water. She wanted to drink and drink. She wanted to hold him, touch him, tell him how much she loved and needed him. But the last month had taught a bitter lesson, and so, even as his kiss deepened, she abruptly drew away and tremblingly turned to look out across the square.

'When—when did you get back?' she asked unsteadily, trying to keep her voice light.

For a moment he didn't answer and she could feel his eyes on her, then he said calmly, 'About a week ago.'

'A week—and yet you say you missed me?' The bitterness was out now, hard and brittle.

Putting his hands on her shoulders, Leo turned her round to face him. She tried to shake off his hands, to resist him, but he wouldn't let go. Firmly he said, 'Yes, a week. But I haven't been in London. I had to go to my company's headquarters in the Midlands to be filled in on my next assignment. There didn't seem to be any point in calling you until I could see you.'

'You know where you're going?' Despite all her resolutions Gael just had to ask, had to know where he would be.

'Yes. I'm being sent to Bali, in Indonesia. They're building a vast new hospital complex there and I'm to be the Technical Service and Personnel Manager, in charge of the project from start to finish. It will probably take about two years.'

So far, and so long! Gael gazed at him wordlessly, almost wishing that he hadn't come back, hadn't told her that she was going to lose him again for so long. 'When—when will you be leaving?' she managed.

'In about three weeks.'

'I—I see.' She turned away, looking down at her hands as she gripped them together in her lap, trying to tell herself that they had three weeks, three whole weeks, that she would hold and treasure every minute, that she wouldn't spoil it by letting him see how much she cared. She must try and keep it light, emotion-free. Determinedly she raised her head and tried to smile, tried to say, 'Well, we'll have to make them fun to look back on,' but she found his grey eyes watching her closely, and suddenly the words were gone and she could only look at him helplessly, her despair in her face, until she lowered her head, unable to bear it any longer.

And then, hardly able to credit her own senses, she heard him say firmly, 'I want to take you with me. It doesn't give you much time, I know, and we'll have to make do with a wedding in a registrar's office, and travel out to Bali almost immediately, but I've made sure that ...'

But Gael interrupted him, her eyes very wide in a face that was suddenly transformed. 'What—what did you say?'

Leo's mouth twisted in amusement. 'I said that I'm going to marry you and take you out to Bali with me.' His left eyebrow rose. 'You do *want* to marry me, don't you?'

Gael stared at him for a long moment, then said hastily, 'Yes. Yes, I do.'

'Good.' Quite matter-of-factly, as if proposing marriage was an everyday occurrence, he went on, 'I've arranged with my company to have a furnished house waiting for us and there will be other Europeans there, of course, so you won't feel too much on your own. I've never been to Bali before, but I understand that it's quite civilised.'

He went on talking about the island, but Gael wasn't listening; she just looked at him, radiance in her eyes and filling her body with an overwhelming glow of happiness. But presently she put out a hand and shook his arm so that he stopped and looked at her questioningly.

'Hey! Aren't you going to kiss me?' she demanded.

'Just now, you didn't seem as if you wanted to be kissed,' he said rather wryly.

'That was—that was before,' she said inadequately.

'Oh, I see. I was being punished, was I?'

Gently he drew her into his arms and Gael gazed into his face, her lips already parted for his kiss. Her heart throbbed with intense excitement, for now there was no need to hold back, she could give everything he asked of her, and she had so much to give, so very much. 'Oh, Leo, I love you, I love you,' she whispered as his lips took hers.

He kissed her gently, but soon, too soon, lifted his head to smile down at her. Reaching into the inside pocket of his jacket, he said, 'Here, I've something for you,' and dropped a small box into her hands.

Slowly, almost afraid, Gael opened it and then gasped as she saw the ring inside, an oval sapphire surrounded by diamonds that shone brilliantly against its bed of dark velvet. She couldn't say a word, could only look at Leo with eyes wet with tears of utter joy and happiness.

Taking the ring from the box, he slipped it on to the third finger of her left hand, then gave that slightly mocking smile of his and said blandly, 'Well, I did *say* I'd give you a ring when I got back!'

Gael had never known time to go so quickly; the three weeks passed in a frenzied haze of activity as they made arrangements for the wedding and the journey to Bali. Leo transferred a sum of money that took her breath away into her account and told her to buy everything she wanted for her trousseau and that she thought they might need in the house, so she indulged in an orgy of shopping that was at once intensely satisfying and extremely exhausting. The clothes she bought were mostly for light, summer wear as Leo had told her that it could get pretty hot on the island, and these she packed into a set of new suitcases, but the things for the house: linen, china, cutlery etc., together with her painting equipment and personal belongings, all had to be crated up ready to be flown out after them.

Fortunately Leo sent someone from his firm to take charge of that, while he himself offered to see about a passport for her in her married name as his own would run out during his time in Bali so he also needed a new one. This in the few hurried hours he was able to be with her in London; most of the time he was in the Midlands, putting into operation the first steps in the giant assignment he had undertaken. He even missed the farewell party that the gallery gave for her, which was a big disappointment. But Gael could be philosophical about it now; in just a few days they would be together for the rest of their lives, so she was able to bear being apart for just a little longer.

Leo kissed her often during those three weeks, of course, but seldom anything more than the light, almost brotherly kisses he had given her at the start of their relationship. Gael realised that he was holding back for her sake, that he didn't want to spoil anything for her, but she couldn't help wishing that he would let slip his iron control just a little and show her just how much she meant to him. But he evidently intended to wait until they were married, and really she was content to do so too. It would be far more wonderful to look back on a honeymoon in Bali rather than a hurried pre-marital encounter in the single bed in her flat, she told herself with wry amusement. And it wouldn't be long now, only a few days.

But contrarily those days seemed to drag like lead until at last Gael drove up to the registrar's office with Velma and Clive on the last day of Leo's leave and she saw him waiting for her, wearing a dark suit and looking tall and handsome and very, very dear. Apart from her sister and brother-in-law, she had invited only a few friends to the wedding and Leo had only an old school friend to act as best man, so there were few of them to drink the champagne at the wedding breakfast that Leo had arranged at a nearby hotel. But Gael couldn't have cared less how many people were there; she opened presents, cut the cake, posed for photographs, smiling and joining in the laughter and conversation, but was only really aware of Leo standing so close beside her, his arm negligently round her waist, or his hand under her elbow. She couldn't believe that they were really married, that she belonged to him, and he to her. She didn't even feel any different. But perhaps that would come later, when they were alone together. The shining new wedding ring on her finger caught her eye and she touched it gently; at least that was different, that was tangible. She glanced up and caught Leo watching her. The dark, brooding look was back in his eyes and she felt a sudden cold shiver of fear, but then it was as if the shutter of a camera clicked and the look was gone as he smiled and came over to her.

Bending his head, he said softly, 'Did I tell you that you make a very beautiful bride?' He took her hands and raised them to his lips as she flushed softly, her eyes misty with love, the fear of the moment before forgotten. 'I'm afraid it's time to say our goodbyes and leave if we don't want to miss the plane,' he added.

Gael nodded and for a moment her hands tightened on his as the thought came to her that she was leaving behind everything she had ever known. But it didn't matter. Nothing mattered except the overwhelming love she felt for the man beside her.

The goodbyes were quickly said, with a special, tearful hug from Velma, and then the drive through the speeding traffic to the airport before they boarded the plane for the long, long flight to Bali. Leo advised her to get as much sleep as she could on the flight, but although she dozed often, Gael was unable to sleep properly and was glad of the refuelling stops when she could stretch her legs while they waited for other passengers to unload and load. She envied Leo his ability to relax completely on the plane, either sleeping, watching the film, or reading the guide book of Bali he had bought for the journey, but even he seemed to become more tense and silent as they took off from Singapore for the last leg of the long trip. If anything, Gael supposed he was thinking of the challenging job that lay ahead of him—heaven knew it was daunting enough, but somehow he had never struck her as being the type that worried about a problem before it manifested itself. But then another possibility occurred to her that brought a flush of colour to her cheeks; after all, it was his wedding night too.

The big jet bounced gently down at Ngurah Rai airport and with a small sigh of relief Gael stepped out of the plane into the brilliant late afternoon sunshine and eighty-degree heat of Bali. Her first sight of the place was disappointing, for the airport buildings were in the same late twentieth-century concrete style as every other airport in the world and there was the usual long wait for their luggage before they could clear Customs. But in the reception area they were approached by a middle-aged man in a lightweight suit who introduced himself as Malcolm Taylor, the company agent on the island.

'Welcome to Bali,' he greeted them. 'How was the flight? Here, let me take some of these cases. I've got a car waiting outside.'

He led the way out of the airport and held the back door of the car for Gael. She slid in as the man stowed the luggage, but felt a sharp stab of surprise and disappointment as Leo got into the front seat beside Malcolm Taylor. Then she smiled slightly to herself, realising that being put firmly in the back seat was a thing that happened to wives. A wife—how strange to think of herself as that! Mrs Leo Kane. She tried the title out in her mind and found that she liked it very much. For twenty-two years she had been Gael Markham, but now no one would ever call her by that name again. She glanced at Leo, already deep in conversation about the hospital project, and her heart seemed to

swell and want to burst with love and longing. If only he
would ... But perhaps tonight, when they were alone together at last, surely then he would tell her that he loved
her.

But once outside the airport complex all thoughts of the
coming night faded as they turned north and headed inland. Her guide book had told Gael that the islands of
Indonesia were originally known as the Spice Islands and
she had expected to see a certain amount of cultivation, but
nothing had prepared her for the mile upon mile of terraced
rice fields that stretched in great curving lines of brilliant
green colour across the landscape.

'Good heavens, they seem to go on for ever!' she exclaimed.

Malcolm broke off something he was saying to Leo and
half turned towards her. 'The Balinese call them the giant
staircases to heaven. The name for a rice field is *sawah*, and
those curving lines are earth walls which retain the water
from the irrigation system. You can always tell how the
rice is growing because when the fields are flooded the
plants are young and when they're dry the rice is ready for
harvesting.'

His tone was rather patronising, as if he was giving a
lecture, but Gael didn't mind, she sat forward in her seat
and gazed out of the window, drinking in the new sights:
the slight, brown-skinned men, naked except for a sarong-
like garment tied round their waists and a straw coolie hat
to keep off the sun, pounding the rice with hoe-like tools,
and here and there a boy, almost hidden under his huge hat,
guided a flock of ducks across the fields with the aid of a
very long pole with a piece of rag flapping on the end. He
only had to make a slight movement of the pole and the

ducks all turned in the direction he wanted like a platoon of well-trained soldiers.

Gael gave a little chuckle of delight and turned to Leo, her face alight with eagerness and excitement. For a moment their eyes met, then he immediately turned away and spoke to Malcolm again.

They drove through the big, modern town of Denpasar, a town so packed with people and with so many new sights that Gael could hardly take them all in and it was almost a relief to leave the town behind as they headed east towards the coast. Malcolm was explaining that they had been assigned a bungalow, one of several in a small estate that the company had taken over for the use of its executive staff.

'There are already quite a few Europeans from other Western companies living there and we've got quite a nice social circle going,' he told them. 'I took the liberty of asking my wife to hire some servants for you so that you'd have everything waiting for you,' he added. 'They don't live-in but will come every day.'

The bungalow, when they at last pulled up outside it, was a new building of Western design, but with the roof overhanging to give a veranda all the way round. As soon as the car stopped a middle-aged couple, their gentle faces big with smiles of welcome, came hurrying out to greet them.

'This is Pak Amat and his wife Kartini; they do speak English,' Malcolm told them.

But to his and Gael's surprise, Leo turned to the Indonesian couple and spoke to them in their own language, which made the smiles even wider and their ducking bows more frequent.

'I didn't know you could speak Indonesian,' Gael remarked as he picked up one of the cases and took her arm to lead her inside.

He looked amused. 'What do you think I've been doing for the last three weeks?'

Malcolm followed them in. 'You should find everything you want here, but if you need anything just give me a ring, we're not far away,' he said as he offered Leo his card.

'Thanks. We appreciate all you've done for us. I'll telephone you and let you know when I'll be ready to visit the site.' It was said politely and without any undue emphasis, but that one sentence established that Leo was taking over from now on, and it was with a rather deflated air that Malcolm Taylor said his goodbyes and left.

Pak Amat stood ready to show them round the house: he wore a white sarong with a white shirt, loose like a jacket over it, and a white cloth bound round his dark hair, rather like a turban with a hole in it. With great pride he pointed out the television set and the radio in the sitting-room, and snapped the lights on and off several times to show that they worked. He also ran all the taps in the bathroom to prove that water came out of them. 'We do not have to fetch water from the river,' he told them in his broken English. There was also a dining-room and two bedrooms, one quite a bit larger than the other and with a breathtaking view out over the palm-strewn coastline.

Gael turned impulsively to Leo. 'Let's have this room, shall we?' and then blushed furiously.

But Leo merely nodded and said something to Pak Amat in Indonesian. There was a brief exchange and Leo said, 'It seems we're now to view the kitchen.'

Here Kartini took over the guided tour and they duly admired the water taps over the sink and the new electric cooker, on which was simmering a saucepan that emitted the most delicious smell and reminded Gael that she had only had airline food for two days and had been too pent up with nervous excitement to eat properly for some time before that.

Kartini, who was dressed similarly to her husband, but far more colourfully and with a bright sash tied round her waist, said, 'When you wish eat, please?'

'I think a shower and a change of clothes first, don't you?' Leo asked, and Gael gave a heartfelt nod of agreement. 'Okay, you take the bathroom first.'

The water was lukewarm and she couldn't seem to make it hotter or colder, but it was heavenly to stand in the shower and feel the grubbiness of the journey wash away and then to change into clean clothes, a deep gold coloured dress because she knew it suited her and because Leo had once told her she looked lovely when she had worn a blouse in that colour. She heard him moving about in the bathroom and then go into the other bedroom to change. She looked around the room with its large double bed and could hardly believe that she was here in Bali, that she was married, and that soon she would be sharing the bed with Leo. Nervous tension gripped her and the eyes that looked back at her from the dressing-table mirror were wide and dark-smudged in her pale face. Hey, this wouldn't do! Carefully she applied make-up to cover the smudges of tiredness and sprayed on some of the madly expensive French perfume she had lashed out on especially for tonight. Then she examined herself in the long mirror. Yes, she would pass. Her hair fell in shining waves to her shoulders, the dress clung in all the right places. So why did she suddenly feel very young, very afraid?

Angrily she shook off the mood and went into the sitting-room. Leo was already there, dressed in a dark grey suit that she hadn't seen before.

'It seems Taylor thought of everything,' he remarked, and handed her a dry Martini that he had already poured for her.

The meal was delicious—rice of course, but Gael found that even though she was hungry she couldn't do justice to the meal, she was much too tense and nervous, and took refuge in talking animatedly about the sights they had seen on their journey from the airport, but her voice sounded brittle even to her own ears. And Leo was unusually silent, which made it seem worse; most times he was an amusing and knowledgeable companion, ready to talk on any topic she brought up, but tonight he was taciturn, answering only when she asked him a direct question, the rest of the time gazing down at his glass, twisting the red wine in it round and round between his fingers, he too not eating very much.

After the meal they sat on the veranda in the warm darkness until the Indonesian couple bade them a soft good-night and left for their own home.

Gael waited for a few minutes and then rose. 'I think I'll go in now. Are you—are you coming?' she asked as steadily as she could.

'No, you go ahead. I think I'll have another cigarette first.'

Gael used the bathroom and then went into the bedroom, and immediately she did so the feelings of fear and vulnerability came rushing back. Leo seemed so strange to-night. Was he regretting bringing her with him? She wanted so much to please him, but she was so young, so inexperienced. The twelve-year age gap had seemed unimportant before, but when you compared his undoubted sophistication with her complete innocence ... But he *had* brought her here, and he *had* married her, and that was all that mattered. And after tonight—well, she wouldn't be quite so inexperienced any more. She undressed and put on a long black lace nightdress with matching negligee that had cost what seemed to be a small fortune at the time, but which was worth every penny, she now decided as she stood before the mirror and brushed her hair in the soft glow given off by the bedside lamps.

Behind her the door opened and Leo came into the room. With trembling fingers she put down the hairbrush and turned to face him. He was standing just inside the door, watching her, still fully dressed. The strange, cold look was back on his face again and he made no move to go to her or to speak.

Gael gazed at him uncertainly. Well, if he wouldn't come to her ... Without giving herself time to hesitate, she quickly crossed the room and reached up to put her arms round his neck. Her voice dry in her throat, she said with a nervous little laugh, 'Pak Amat has put all your things in the other room; we'll have to tell him to move them to-morrow.'

For a long moment Leo continued to gaze down at her, then he deliberately reached up and pulled her arms from round his neck and pushed her away from him as if she was something dirty.

'That won't be necessary. I have no intention of sharing this room with you.'

Gael stared at him in amazement. 'I—I don't understand. You mean you—you want a room of your own?'

His mouth curled and he looked at her as if he despised

her. 'I mean that I have no intention of consummating this marriage,' he answered contemptuously.

'But—but why? What have I done?' The words came out on a sob of dazed bewilderment.

'I'll tell you what you've done,' he said with sudden savagery as if he could no longer control himself. 'You killed the girl I loved, the girl I was going to marry! You went to your drunken little party and drove a car you couldn't control and you killed her! You killed her!'

CHAPTER THREE

GAEL stared at him in appalled horror. His words had stabbed like knife thrusts into her brain, but she still couldn't believe that this was happening to her. But it was his eyes that made her believe; they were dark with hatred and with a torment that had been too long suppressed.

'No! Oh, please God, no!' But even as she instinctively sobbed out the prayer she knew that it was hopeless, that nothing would ever bring back the peace and happiness of a few moments ago. Her life was wrecked, now and for always. But even though she knew it was useless, she still tried to fight. 'Leo, that isn't true. I didn't kill her! It wasn't my fault.'

His lips curled contemptuously. 'And now you're going to prove what a rotten, hypocritical little cheat you are by trying to wriggle out of your responsibility by saying that it was only an accident.'

Her face ashen, Gael stared into his taut face. She knew

then that nothing she could say, now or ever, would convince him that he was wrong. He had fed his grief with hatred and she would never be able to make him change his mind. What was the point in denying it, in telling him that she hadn't even been driving that night?

In a voice that was little more than a painful whisper, she said, 'Why? Why did you bring me here? Marry me?'

'Because to take on this job I needed to be married. You'd robbed me of a wife, but I didn't see why you should rob me of the job I wanted as well,' he answered viciously. 'You'd ruined my every hope of happiness, but I was damned if I was going to let you ruin my career!' His eyes glared down at her as he jeeringly said the words that turned Gael's heart to stone. 'So I found out from the court records where you lived and followed you to the gallery. The rest was easy,' he went on, his lip curling disdainfully. 'You almost begged to fall into my net. The only difficulty I had was in not letting you see how much you disgusted me—and in keeping you at arm's length until I was ready to make use of you.'

Gael saw it all then, saw how his grief must have twisted his mind and made him decide to take his resentment and anger at his loss out on her. But to marry her! To make her believe that he cared about her! Suddenly her legs refused to support her and she slumped down on the bed, her hands shaking now with entirely different emotions from those of earlier in the evening. Her eyes dark in her haggard face, she said in a hoarse voice that she didn't recognise as her own, 'You can't do this to me. You have no right to ...'

'No right?' Leo made a sudden lunge and pulled her roughly to her feet, his fingers biting into the soft flesh of her upper arms. In a fury he snarled, 'You say I have no right? Well I'll tell you... So help me, my conscience did smite me that weekend we went sailing together. I considered then chucking in the whole idea and walking out of your life, because you seemed so—but that doesn't matter. I decided to give you a chance, and so I deliberately made you talk about the accident. And you said it was nothing! Nothing!' He shook her, his hands bruising her until she gave a little stifled sob. 'You dismissed the whole incident as if it was some trifling annoyance that wasn't worth talking about. And that was when I finally decided to go ahead and make you pay for what you've done to me!'

For a moment longer his eyes blazed into hers, then he let her go so suddenly that she collapsed on to the bed, her senses reeling and hardly aware that he had turned on his heel and strode abruptly from the room, slamming the door behind him.

She lay where she was for a long time, a crumpled heap of flowing golden hair and black lace upon the white counterpane. At first she felt too numb, too shocked, to cry, but then the tears came in great heaving sobs and she turned to bury her face in the pillows, her biggest fear that Leo would hear her and derive satisfaction from her misery. She cried until there were no tears left, but even then her body shook with silent, convulsive sobs and when daylight crept into the room she still lay there, her eyes dark and sunken in her ashen face as she stared into a future of blackness and despair.

When it was still very early Gael heard soft noises from the kitchen and realised that the servants had arrived. Slowly she sat up, but then caught sight of herself in the dressing-table mirror. Despair turned then to sudden, uncontrollable rage and with fierce strength she took hold of the nightdress and negligee and tore them off, taking her wretchedness out on the garments she had put on in such trembling anticipation such a short time ago—a lifetime ago, when she had been a happy bride instead of a woman rejected by the man she loved in the cruellest way imaginable. She sat naked, her head in her hands, until sheer exhaustion made her crawl between the cool sheets and she fell into a troubled, unrestful sleep.

It was the nightmare that woke her again, brought her to her senses with a moan of terror on her lips, her body hot and shaking. For a few seconds she couldn't think where she was, but then she saw the tattered remnants of black lace lying in a shaft of sunlight on the floor and she remembered —everything. For a moment she closed her eyes in agony and wished she were dead, that she had never been born. She couldn't go on living, not like this, she couldn't stand it! How could she face even seeing Leo again, knowing that he hated her, that he had never loved her? Despair gripped her heart. She just wanted to curl up into a ball and die.

But it was so hot! The air in the room was stifling and she was dripping with perspiration, the sheet beneath her sticking damply to her body. Thrusting back the covers, Gael got out of bed and groped her way to the window. As she pulled back the curtains the strong sunlight almost blinded her and she realised that it was low in the sky; she must have slept through most of the day. For a little while after she opened the windows the fresh air was a blessed relief, but the atmosphere was still very humid and did nothing to cool her fevered body or lift the hair that clung damply to her head. The only answer was a shower, but every nerve shrank from leaving the sanctuary of her room.

Suppose she saw Leo? How on earth could she face him? But gradually her need to get cool forced her to put on a bathrobe and with trembling hands open the door. The house was very quiet, she couldn't hear a sound. Her confidence increasing a little, she opened the door wider and ran the few yards to the bathroom, slipping inside and thankfully locking the door behind her.

The shower was beautifully cool and she just stood there and let it pour over her for ages. At one point she saw the red marks on her arms where Leo had shaken her so furiously and that made her cry again, safe in the knowledge that no one would hear her over the noise of the running water. After a long time she turned off the shower and towel-dried her hair, then hugged her robe around her before hurrying back to her room.

She breathed a sigh of relief as she reached it, but then gave a sob of fright as she realised that someone was there. But it was only Kartini who smilingly nodded to her.

'Please, *njonya*, you wish eat now?'

'No!' Gael's nails dug into her palms as she tried to pull herself together. 'No, thank you. I'm not hungry.'

The woman nodded and bent to pick up a pile of soiled bed-linen. She looked uncertainly at Gael. 'Please, you wish——' she paused to grope for the English words, 'you wish air?'

Gael looked at her uncomprehendingly, then noticed that Kartini was pointing to a metal, boxlike object, rather like a night-store heater, attached to the wall. She went over to it and flicked a switch and the contraption immediately began to give out a whining noise. Of course, an air-conditioner! Why on earth hadn't she noticed it before? But there were plenty of reasons, as she bitterly reminded herself. She nodded to Kartini and wished she would go away; all she wanted right now was to be left alone. But the woman was asking her something else as she stooped to indicate the tattered shreds of her nightgown.

'Throw it away,' Gael snapped out. 'Burn it!' Crossing quickly to the window, she stood there until she heard the door close behind Kartini, and then slumped against the wall, feeling ashamed of herself. No matter how wretched she felt it gave her no right to snap at an innocent by-stander. If she was going to snap at anyone it ought to be Leo. But her mind shrank from even the thought of seeing him again. She supposed she ought to be terribly angry at what he had done to her, but the hurt was still too raw for her to feel anything but pain.

Later that day she heard the sound of a car pulling up outside and then Leo's voice speaking to Pak Amat. So there had been no reason to be afraid; he hadn't even been in the house when she had ventured to use the shower. She sat in a chair near the window of her room and watched the sun go down over the terraced hills; you couldn't call it a sunset, it happened far too quickly for that, the great blood-red orb dropping like a thrown ball beyond the horizon and turning the golden day to dusk. At seven Kartini came to tell her in her halting English that dinner was ready, but Gael again said that she wasn't hungry and sat on, watching the lights twinkling out from the houses in the valley.

Two minutes later there was an abrupt knock on the door and Leo strode into the room, snapping on the light as he did so. There had been nothing to stop him barging in on her, there was no lock on her door. Gael blinked and looked quickly away, and to her chagrin found that she was trembling violently.

Leo looked down at her for a moment, then said harshly, 'Kartini says you won't come to dinner?'

Trying desperately to keep her voice steady, Gael said shortly, 'I'm not hungry.'

His tone was contemptuous. 'If you think that this act of self-martyrdom will have any effect on me, you're completely mistaken. I couldn't care less whether you starve yourself or not.'

Slowly she turned to look at him, her eyes dark pools in her chalk-white face. 'Then why are you here?'

His jaw tightened. 'Only children and immature adolescents shut themselves away and sulk because they can't face up to the truth about themselves.' He paused, but when she didn't answer added caustically, 'You can't shut yourself away in here for ever, Gael. Sooner or later you've got to face up to your position and learn to live with it.'

'With you, you mean,' Gael retorted bitterly.

Leo laughed then, a mocking jeer of a laugh as he said, 'Quite.' But the harsh, mirthless sound seemed to trigger off something inside Gael and suddenly she was angry, furiously, gloriously angry. Abruptly she got to her feet and turned to face him.

'Well, that's just where you're wrong,' she said fiercely. 'Because if you think I'm going to stay here you're crazy! You may have duped me into marrying you and coming to Bali with you, but if you think for one minute that I'm going to hang around to let you use me as a replacement for your girl-friend, then *you're* very much mistaken. I'm leaving here first thing in the morning and I'm taking a plane back to England.'

She stood, chest heaving from her outburst, but Leo merely watched her in cool amusement, his mouth twisted into a cynical smile. 'Really? And just how do you intend to leave here?'

'I'll take a taxi, of course.'

'And just what do you intend to pay the driver with—even if you knew how to get a taxi to come here?'

Gael felt a sudden chill douse her heated anger. It was true that she didn't have any Indonesian currency, hadn't any money at all, in fact; she had spent everything she had on clothes in London, confidently expecting Leo to provide for her after their marriage as he had told her not to bother to bring any money with her. And now she knew why. Desperately she said, 'I'll find a way—somehow!'

His brows flickered and he said, coldly, 'Perhaps you might at that. You might even persuade someone at the airport to let you have a ticket on credit.' He paused to lend emphasis to his words, 'But no one is going to let you through the Customs without a passport—and unfortunately you don't happen to have one, do you?'

Gael stared at him. 'What—what do you mean? You can't refuse to give me my passport!'

'Can't I? I assure you I can. But even if I did it wouldn't do you any good. I made sure that I got a joint passport, in both our names, which means that you're unable to travel alone, you can only do so when you accompany me. Male chauvinism at its worst, of course, but there you are, and at times like this it's extremely useful.'

'You—you can't mean to keep me here!' she gasped.

'I can, and I do—for just so long as you're useful to me.'

Appalled, Gael could only gaze at him wordlessly, then she turned away so that she didn't have to see the triumphant look on his face. Unsteadily she said, 'You had it all planned, didn't you? Right from the beginning.'

'I've already said so.'

Gael swung round to face him again, two bright spots of colour on her cheeks. 'But there's one thing you've left out of your twisted calculations.'

Leo gave a slight frown. 'What thing?'

'My reaction to your insane scheming.' She was able to meet his eyes steadily now as she went on, 'You thought that once you'd tricked me into marrying you and got me to Bali with no hope of getting away from you that I'd do what you want. Well, I won't! No way am I going to submit tamely to your plans. I imagine you expect me to docilely play the part of a company wife and give dinner and cocktail parties for your colleagues, act the perfect hostess all the time, but you've picked the wrong person. I won't do it, do you hear me?'

Her voice had risen hysterically, but broke off abruptly as Leo took a quick stride towards her. His hand went to her throat and the other he coiled in her hair, pulling her head back. Gael tried to claw at the hand holding her throat, but he only tightened his grip on her hair so that tears came to her eyes. His eyes glared down at her, dark with menace.

'You'll do exactly as I tell you, you little bitch! *Because you owe me.* You owe me this job and the happiness Julia and I would have had together. Nothing you can do will ever atone for that, but I'm going to make you pay in the only way possible. Do you understand me?'

He pulled her hair again so that she hastily said, 'Yes,' with a little gasp.

'Good. And don't get any fancy ideas about trying to run away or going to someone for help, because I'll only drag you back again, and I'll make your life so miserable you'll wish you'd never been born!' His fingers tightened on her throat and she began to gasp for air as the room started to swim around her.

With ease he forced her to her knees and then let her go, looking down at her grimly. 'And believe me, it would give me great pleasure to be extremely nasty to you.'

Gael's hands went to her neck and she stared up at him. In little more than a whisper she pleaded, 'Leo, please don't be like this. It doesn't have to be this way. We could—we could work something out, come to some arrangement. I know that you're hurt and—and angry now, but surely we can ...' She broke off, trying to find the right words. 'In England we ...'

He interrupted her tersely. 'If you value your skin you won't remind me of England. Do you think I enjoyed having to be with you? Knowing all the time what you'd done and having to be pleasant to you? I had to force myself to touch you, it filled me with revulsion when I had to kiss you to keep you sweet and make sure of you while I visited Julia's parents when you thought I'd gone to Ibiza. God, I was glad to get away; you clung like a strangling vine! Do you think I would even have looked at you after Julia? She was the loveliest creature on this earth.' His voice filled with pain. 'She was so beautiful, so perfect.'

Gael bit her hand, remembering again the dead girl's face.

Leo looked down at her where she knelt in a crumpled heap at his feet. 'And you—you're nothing!'

It was the next day before Gael ventured out of her room again, and then only after she had heard Leo drive away. It seemed that the working day started early here, because he had left before seven, but already the weather was hot and she put on only a thin cotton sundress and a pair of dark glasses to hide behind and to mask the deep-etched shadows round her eyes. Pak Amat brought her breakfast on the terrace, but she still had no appetite and had to force herself to eat; somehow she thought she was going to need all her strength to get through the coming days.

Because last night she had made up her mind that she wasn't going to let Leo terrify her into submission. She had had plenty of time after he had left her to think things through, and she was pretty sure that, despite his threats of violence, he wouldn't actually harm her. She was too much use to him for that, and besides, too many people knew that she was here. The mind-bending thought that if he had been crazy enough to get her here then he might also be crazy enough to kill her if she didn't do what he wanted, she immediately pushed aside. It was a chance she would have to take. But she was in no way cowed enough to stay here and let Leo treat her like dirt for the two or three years it would take to build the hospital complex. No way! Perhaps if she had really caused Julia Symons' death she might have felt guilt-ridden enough to remain a virtual prisoner here, but the fact that she was entirely innocent had brought anger and resentment as well as bitterness for the trick Leo had played on her. And so she was going to fight him, and somehow, somewhere, there had to be a way to regain her freedom.

She first thought of contacting her brother-in-law to ask him to write to Leo and tell him the whole truth, but put the idea instantly aside; Leo would only think that it was a lie made up to get him to let her go. No, there had to be some other way, and it would have to be something she could do herself, here in Bali. Getting to her feet, Gael wandered restlessly down the garden, even in her preoccupation her artist's eye noting the brilliant colours of the exotic plants and shrubs, all of them completely new to her. They formed walls of flowers and blossom between the garden and its neighbours, with a large patio and then a beautifully tended lawn leading down to a tall wooden gate that opened on to a track that ran along the back of the row of bungalows and down to the sea. Gael walked along it towards the sound of breaking surf, the leaves of the tall palm trees making a soft swishing noise in the breeze and casting dancing shadow patterns on the pathway. As she came nearer she heard voices calling to one another and laughing, and when she rounded a bend she saw a group of people on the beach, women mostly, and several small children who were playing at the edge of the water. They were all European and Gael stopped precipitately, unwilling to be seen. She stepped behind the shelter of a bush, thick with heavily scented purple flowers, and watched for a moment. The women sat in the shade and were talking animatedly together while the children built what looked to be an immense sand castle. They were all happy and laughing together.

A violent stab of pure jealousy hit Gael. How *dare* anyone be happy when she was so wretched? How dare these women flaunt their children in front of her when her marriage had been torn apart before it had even begun and she would never know the joy of having children? Because no matter what came of this, even if she got away from Leo tomorrow, never, *never* would she put her trust in a man again! Turning, she ran back along the track and slammed the garden gate behind her, trying to still the agonising waves of misery that threatened to engulf her again. She

fought them down and channelled them instead to fuel her
hatred for Leo. She had heard that love and hate are closely
akin, but hadn't believed it until last night. Until then,
even when he told her he didn't love her and that it was
all a trick, she had gone on loving him because she could
understand what had driven him to do what he did, but
when he had been so scathing, so unbelievably cruel in
telling her what he really thought about her as a person,
love had turned to hate with an intensity that shocked her.

Slowly she went back up the garden, trying vainly to
think of a way of escape, but her mind was too shocked and
tired to come up with anything at all feasible, and eventually she went inside and brought out her sketchpad, trying
to relax and finding some solace in doing a detailed drawing of a spray from a mauve and purple flowered shrub.

A noise from the bungalow made her look up and she
saw a woman stepping through the French doors towards
her, followed by a rather flustered Pak Amat. The woman
was well-built but sufficiently corseted not to be called
plump, in early middle age and dressed as for formal afternoon tea in England, with carefully lacquered hair under a
large straw hat and a double row of pearls.

'How do you do. I'm Norah Taylor, Malcolm's wife.
Thought I'd just drop in and see how you were settling in.'
She sat down in the chair Pak Amat hastily brought for her
and turning to him, said sharply, 'All right, you can go and
bring us some refreshments now—fruit juice and cakes.
And mind that the juice is freshly squeezed.' Then she
turned back to Gael. 'Well now, have you recovered from
your journey? Such a fag, isn't it, that long flight out from
England? I just wish they'd put Concorde on that route so
that you could do it in one day instead of two.'

Gael looked at the woman uncertainly, feeling totally in-

capable of coping with a social call, of pretending that there
was nothing wrong.

But Norah Taylor hardly gave her time to answer before
she swept on, 'You don't know how lucky you are to have
this bungalow, it's quite the largest on the estate. And with
that lovely big lounge—just right for parties. Of course
you'll be giving a lot of those once the rest of the British
personnel for the hospital project start arriving. That's why
I got you Pak Amat and Kartini, they're quite good servants
compared to a lot of the Sudras—that's the Balinese working class, you know,' she added patronisingly, knowing that
Gael knew nothing of the sort. Pak Amat came out then
carrying the tray of refreshments, and her visitor went on,
'But you have to be very firm with them. Don't stand for
any nonsense, because if you're the slightest bit lax they
tend to treat you as one of their family, and that's fatal.'

Gael blushed with embarrassment, knowing that the servant had understood every word, and she hastily avoided
his eyes.

But Mrs Taylor had no such inhibitions and exclaimed
with annoyance, 'Really, Pak Amat, you've left the pips in
this orange juice. Take it away and strain it at once!'

The manservant bowed repeatedly, muttering his apolo-
gies and hurrying away to do her bidding while the older
woman raised her eyebrows in an expression of impatient
resignation. 'You see what I mean? But you'll soon learn
how to handle them. You just have to rule them as children,
really.'

Gael found herself in heartfelt sympathy for any off-
spring that Norah Taylor might have, but politely asked
the expected question, 'Do you have any children, Mrs
Taylor?'

'Oh, please, don't be so formal. We all call each other by

our first names here. Yes, I have two boys. They're both away at school in England at the moment, of course, but they come home for the long summer holidays. Not that they like Bali very much; they're always pleased to go back to England.'

I bet they are! Gael thought, and thanked heaven that she had never been inflicted with such a parent. Pak Amat came back with the orange juice and the woman glared at him, rebuking him again. Gael sat there, tight-lipped, resenting this high-handed bossiness with *her* servants, in *her* house.

Norah, however, seemed immune to Gael's growing tension. 'Malcolm tells me that your husband is a demon for work. He's already got the first workers on the site and is having a temporary site office erected. Does he always work at this speed?'

'I believe he does have a reputation for getting things done,' Gael agreed tightly.

'You believe?' A thinly-plucked eyebrow was raised interrogatively.

Gael cursed herself for a fool. 'We haven't been married very long,' she admitted.

'Why, how wonderful! So you're still a bride?' Norah leaned forward and patted her hand until Gael hastily withdrew it. 'And I expect you're feeling terribly nervous about having to welcome all the new people and entertain them. Well, you don't have to worry about a thing, my dear. I'll take care of everything for you, arrange all the parties and tell you who to invite and point out which people are important and which don't matter. As your husband's in charge of the whole project, you really need only concern yourself with the architects and the various department managers. The lesser staff like the Personnel Officer and the technical officers you need only invite to a cocktail party or something when they first arrive, and then you needn't bother with them any more.'

Gael gazed at her speechlessly, stunned by her arrant snobbishness while she went rambling happily on, obviously envisaging herself as taking over Gael's social duties and leading her along like a willing and rather stupid puppy on a lead.

'Of course,' she was saying, 'you'll have to join our Country Club that all the resident Europeans here belong to. But there won't be any difficulty; Malcolm and I will propose you, and I think I have enough influence to get you in,' she added with a smile that was more of a self-satisfied smirk. 'I'm on the committee, you know, and I'm also President of the women's section. Have been for about three years, actually.'

Only because I bet anyone who tried to oppose you got trampled into the ground, Gael thought acidly. Resentment grew, she had been tricked into coming here by Leo and now Norah Taylor was trying to manipulate her. Well, Gael had had quite enough of being jerked around like a puppet on a string, thank you very much. Coldly she said, 'Please don't bother to propose me for your Club. I'm not sure that we'll want to join.'

The plucked eyebrows rose superciliously and then Norah gave a condescending laugh. 'My dear Gael, *everyone* who is anyone joins the Country Club. It's the only civilised place to go to. There's a pool, and tennis courts and ...'

'Aren't there any Balinese places to go to?' Gael interrupted brusquely.

Norah raised her eyebrows in horror. 'One doesn't mix with the natives! Oh, of course we sometimes watch their festivals because they're so quaint and colourful, and because of Malcolm's position we sometimes have to attend functions given by the Indonesian government, but one doesn't mix with them socially on a day-to-day basis, we stay within the British community for that—or, at least, the English-speaking community, because there are a lot of Australians here.' She leaned forward and added earnestly, 'I don't think you quite understand your position here, my dear. As the wife of the Project Manager you hold a very high position in the social hierarchy.' She gave a false, trilling little laugh. 'Oh, I daresay that seems very old-fashioned to someone as young as you, but I assure you it's still terribly important in such an out-of-the-way place as this. And your behaviour, of course, rebounds on your husband. And I'm sure you want to do your best for him and help him to rise even higher in his company. I understand that if he does well with this project then the next step will be a directorship.'

Gael stared at her. 'How do you know that? Did Leo tell you?'

'Good heavens, no! I haven't met your husband yet, although I'm so looking forward to it. No, it was just something one hears on the grapevine, you know.' She paused and looked at Gael consideringly. 'Your husband must be quite a good deal older than you?'

'Yes, he is,' Gael agreed shortly.'

'And you? How old are you, my dear?'

Gael was so taken aback by the personalness of the question that she answered automatically. 'Twenty-two.'

'So young! Good heavens, what I wouldn't give to be

twenty-two again,' said with a false laugh that belied her words. She was far too complacently enjoying the power of her maturity. 'But you mustn't be afraid, you know. I'll take you under my wing and make sure you don't make any mistakes. We wouldn't want to disappoint that new husband of yours, would we?'

Gael stayed silent, the reminder of her youth suddenly making her feel very lost and vulnerable again. Perhaps she was wrong about Norah Taylor, perhaps she did genuinely want just to help her. For a moment she considered confiding in her, asking her to help her to get away from Leo. She looked down at her hands, tight-fisted in her lap, trying to find the words.

But before she could speak, Norah reached out to pick up her sketch-pad. 'Oh, I see you draw. Why, that's quite good. That's bougainvillaea, you know,' she added, indicating the spray of blossom.

'No, I didn't know,' Gael answered slowly.

'Why, how convenient! We're always on the lookout for someone to do little drawings for the posters and programmes and that sort of thing for the Women's Club. It will give you something to do in your spare time. Yes, I think you're going to be quite useful,' she finished on a note of satisfaction.

Something seemed to harden in Gael's brain. The disparagement of her painstaking art work as 'a little drawing' changed resentment into resolve. All thoughts of asking for help dissolved under the determination not to be pushed around any longer. Icily she said, 'I'm afraid you'll have to find someone else to make your posters. I have no intention of joining your Club or any of its sub-sections. And thank you for your offer, but I'm quite capable of arranging my own parties—should I choose to give any.'

'Well, really!' Norah Taylor stared at her as if she'd suddenly grown horns. Then she got angrily to her feet. 'I don't think you know quite what you're turning down, young lady. You won't get very far here without my help, you know. At the moment you're just a little nobody fresh out from England, but ...'

That did it! Gael had been denigrated enough already by Leo without anyone else adding their mite. She got up and walked across to the house, Mrs Taylor having perforce to follow her. Pak Amat came at Gael's call.

'Mrs Taylor is just leaving. Will you show her out, please?'

The older woman drew herself up. 'I'll have you know I came here to invite you and your husband to dinner tonight, but after this I ...'

'We have another engagement,' Gael broke in brusquely.

'But you've only just got here.'

'We're engaged indefinitely.'

'Well! Of all the nerve! You impudent little upstart!' Norah Taylor gazed at her incredulously, completely amazed that anyone could so openly defy her. Then she gave a nasty, brittle laugh, 'Well, you may think you're too high and mighty for us, but I wonder how long that will last when your husband hears about this!' With which parting shot she turned on her high heels and stalked out, nose in the air, the picture of injured indignation.

When the manservant had seen her out, Gael called him back. 'Pak Amat, if that woman or anyone else calls you are to say that I'm out. Do you understand?'

Comprehension was the last thing in Pak Amat's face, but he answered dutifully, 'Yes, *njonya*, I understand.'

Gael turned and walked back into the garden, and realised suddenly that she had struck the first blow in her own defence. Leo might be able to force her to stay here, but there was no way he could force her to take on the duties of his wife if she refused to do so. And if he did try to compel her then it would be a simple thing to behave so badly that it created a scandal. Why, he might even be taken off the project and recalled to London, with all the disgrace that would entail. Hope began to run through her veins. Perhaps she had already found the way out. It wouldn't do her reputation any good, of course, but that was a small price to pay to be free of Leo Kane for ever!

CHAPTER FOUR

HIS anger penetrated to her even before he entered the house. Gael was in her room, rearranging some of her clothes when she heard the car turn into the drive and pull up sharply, the door slamming behind Leo as he ran up the steps on to the veranda. A snapped-out question to Pak Amat and then his quick strides down the corridor towards her room. For a moment her heart fluttered with fear, but then she took hold of her new resolve and turned a cold but calm face to meet him.

He thrust the door open and stood glaring at her for a second before taking a purposeful step into the room and pushing it shut behind him.

Gael leapt to the attack. 'Get out of my room,' she ordered before he could speak. 'Don't you dare touch me!'

But she might just as well not have bothered. Leo strode across and caught her arm, spinning her round. 'Just what the hell do you think you're playing at? I've had Malcolm Taylor in my office bleating that you'd insulted his wife.'

Gael glared back at him triumphantly. 'Yes, I did! And I shall go on insulting your colleagues and their wives until you either let me go or else your company gets so disgusted with my behaviour that they take you off this project. I shouldn't wonder if they don't even ask you to resign,' she added fiercely.

Leo had let go of her arm, was standing looking down at her, his eyes narrowed. His overt anger seemed to have gone but was replaced by a menace that made her suddenly afraid again. Far from being put out he seemed almost amused.

'So that's your little game, is it? How obliging of you to tell me. So you really think you can defy me?' He laughed grimly. 'It seems that I didn't give you a big enough lesson yesterday, or perhaps it's just that you're even more stupid than I thought.' Almost casually he reached up to wind his hand in her hair and pushed her down on to the bed, pressing her face down hard into the soft covers.

Gael struggled, trying to kick out at him, but he was so much stronger than her that her fight was inevitably brief. When he at last pulled her to her feet she swayed and would have fallen if he hadn't caught hold of her.

He was breathing rather heavily and there was a look of grim satisfaction in his eyes. He knew that he'd won, that she had no fight left in her. But the feel of his hands on her bare arm brought her crashing back to awareness and she recoiled from his touch, pulling herself away and standing alone, her head bowed, not looking at him.

His voice harsh, Leo said, 'That's better. You can think up as many little schemes as you like, but there's no way that you can fight me and win. If you try it, by being rude to my colleagues or any other way, then I'll just have to give you another lesson, and a far more unpleasant one,' he added threateningly. 'And if you think you can appeal to anyone for help, forget it. I've already told Malcolm Taylor that you've been ill and aren't yourself yet, that you're still liable to behave irrationally at times.' His voice became silky. 'They'll all feel very sorry for you, and won't believe a word of anything you tell them. But they'll feel even sorrier for me, saddled with a wife who has a persecution complex and makes up such dreadful lies about me. They'll all be on my side, Gael, especially when they see what a devoted husband I am to you, always at your side, hardly letting you out of my sight.'

He moved towards her, but Gael shrank away. 'Don't come near me! Don't touch me!'

'All right.' He looked at her drooping figure contemptuously. 'I don't want to touch you any more than I have to. Now, get changed. We're going to the Taylors for dinner. And when we get there you'll apologise to Mrs Taylor for your behaviour this afternoon. Won't you?' he added menacingly as he saw the flash of resentment in her eyes.

Gael bit her lip and turned away. 'Yes, all right.'

'Good. Put on something sophisticated.' His eyes narrowed and he said softly, 'And if I find that you haven't obeyed me then I'll come in here and dress you myself, do you understand?'

She looked at him wide-eyed, the words, You wouldn't dare, almost on her lips, but the coldly triumphant gleam in his dark eyes told her what she knew already; that he would, that he would do anything he damn well wanted to!

He gave a brief, satisfied nod. 'I see you do understand.' Then he turned and left her alone with her humiliation.

The evening at the Taylors' house couldn't have been worse from Gael's point of view. Leo was all smooth charm from the moment they entered the door, apologising for her behaviour, which he put down to nerves due to a combination of her recent supposed illness and jet-lag. Talk about pouring oil on troubled waters; he soon had Norah Taylor purring like a contented cat by his calculated charm and flattery, so that in only a little while she was saying, Oh, it was nothing, and she wasn't one to take offence at a young girl's gaucheness.

'That's very sweet of you,' said Leo, smiling at Norah warmly, his gaze admiring. 'But I know that Gael wants to apologise for any misunderstanding herself, don't you, darling?'

Darling! Of all the hypocritical, low-down ...

He put an arm round Gael's waist and propelled her forward. When she didn't speak at once he pressed his fingers hard into her side, still smiling silkily.

Gael gave a little gasp and managed a travesty of a smile. 'I'm sorry if you were offended this afternoon.' And you can take that how you like, she thought defiantly.

But Norah chose to be gracious. 'Think nothing of it, my dear. I had no idea you'd been ill. But we must try to be friends in future, mustn't we? And I want you to know that you can call on me any time, for any help you need,' she added for Leo's benefit, smiling up at him like a conspirator. 'Now, you must come along and meet my other guests.'

She led them into the sitting-room where they found two other couples already talking over their aperitifs. And Gael knew immediately, from the way they all looked at her first instead of Leo, their faces openly curious, that Norah had already related the details of their meeting that afternoon. For a moment Gael hesitated, but Leo's hand came beneath her elbow and stayed there until all the introductions were carried out and they were given their glasses of sherry.

The two other couples were a Dr Tom Stanton and his wife Moira, who, Gael gathered, ran a small private hospital for the local Europeans and any visiting tourists who happened to be taken ill while holidaying in the area, and Jane and Mark Ellis, who were friends of the Taylors, the husband being the representative for a large American concern. They were all considerably older than Gael, although Leo seemed to have no difficulty in finding a conversational level with them.

At dinner she was placed between Malcolm Taylor and Tom Stanton with Leo, fortunately, at the other end of the table being monopolised by Norah, who was extolling the delights of her precious Country Club. Malcolm spoke politely to her, but with some reserve, but Gael answered only in monosyllables and felt relieved when he turned to talk to Jane Ellis on his other side. But after the first course Dr Stanton gave her a friendly smile and asked her whereabouts in England she came from. He was more patient than Malcolm Taylor; used to having to exert his bedside manner, Gael supposed, and she tried to respond to his kindness, but felt too miserable to really care, lapsing into silence and wishing that the wretched evening would soon be over.

There was air-conditioning in the room, but the food was spicy and Gael began to feel hot. She was wearing a black sequin-covered evening jacket over a sleeveless cocktail dress, black again, and gathered in soft folds that crossed quite low at the front and fell into a straight skirt. She leaned forward to take off the jacket and Tom Stanton turned to help her.

'Hallo, you've been in the wars,' he remarked. 'That's quite a set of bruises you've got on your arm.'

Gael glanced down at where he was looking and felt herself go pale. The marks of Leo's fingers, where he had held her and shaken her so angrily, showed clearly, livid blue patches on her white skin. Instinctively she looked at Leo and found him watching her, daring her to say anything.

'Oh, I—it's nothing. I knocked into a shelf,' she managed lamely, which was as much a salve to her own pride as fear.

But Tom Stanton was looking at Leo and then slowly back to examine her arm again. His eyes came up to meet her frightened ones and then he turned away and began to talk to the neighbour on his other side. But in that glance Gael had seen that he knew; he was a doctor and wasn't to be fooled by a feeble lie.

The evening seemed to drag on as if it would never end, the talk increasing and the laughter becoming louder as everyone consumed more of the imported French wine. Gael's head began to throb and her hand was shaking as she lifted her glass to sip her drink, although the food she hardly touched because it seemed to make her hotter and thirstier. She would have loved a long drink of ice-cold water, but was afraid of drawing attention to herself by asking for it. They had given up trying to draw her out, even Dr Stanton, and she was thankful to just sit and long for the evening to come to an end. She looked across the table to where Leo sat next to his hostess. He looked extremely handsome in a white tuxedo that she hadn't seen him wear before; it accentuated his tan and the gleam of his white, even teeth as he smiled at Norah Taylor who was leaning towards him so that he could look down her cleavage, her cheeks flushed and her voice shrill as she related some anecdote about how she, as president, had dealt with some native servant problem at her famous Club. She was openly making up to Leo, almost flirting with him, and purring with pleasure every time he smiled or said something admiring.

Gael felt a surge of contempt for the woman's obvious behaviour, but it was instantly shattered as she remembered how, just a short while ago, she too had blossomed under Leo's smiles, had sparkled because she was the centre of his attention and he made her feel as if she was the only woman in the world. A great stab of jealousy shook her and she gripped her glass until her knuckles showed white, but the feeling was quickly dispelled. Leo's attentions to Norah were as false as they had been to her.

He must have felt her watching him, because he turned and met her eyes. For a moment his face grew hard with hate, then the look changed to a mixture of malicious triumph and contempt before he again turned back to listen to Norah. With shaking hand, Gael lifted up her glass and drank the rest of the contents in one swallow. The wine was too dry and she didn't really like it, but she welcomed the numbness it brought to her brain, the way it dimmed reality, and she looked round to have her glass refilled, but over her head Dr Stanton said something to the servant and shortly afterwards a glass of lemonade was quietly put in front of her.

'You look a little flushed,' Tom said matter-of-factly. 'Which isn't surprising when you're not used to a tropical climate. One tends to get dehydrated if one isn't careful.'

Gael accepted the drink gratefully, but as he went on talking easily to her without expecting her to answer, she wondered just how much he had seen and what conclusions he had drawn. And then realised bitterly that she didn't much care anyway. She wished she was anywhere but here, she wished she were dead!

After a lifetime it broke up at last and for a few minutes it was bliss to walk out into the open, but then the humid air closed round her again and she felt hot and sticky. She said goodbye hurriedly, but Leo was taking ages to say goodnight, thanking the Taylors, laughingly accepting other invitations. Abruptly Gael walked away and got in the car, slamming the door.

There was a brief silence in the doorway and then, through the open window, she heard Leo say clearly, 'I know you'll all forgive Gael. The poor darling's still far from well and I'm afraid it will take her a while to recover from the long journey. I'd have spared her it if I could, but there wasn't time for a leisurely sea voyage, unfortunately. And I couldn't possibly have let her make the trip alone.'

There was a concerted murmur of commiseration and then Leo came to join her, waving a casual farewell to the others, while Gael seethed with indignation. How dared he give everyone the impression that she was a chronic neurotic —and with suicidal tendencies too, if they cared to read meaning into his last remark! It wasn't far to the bungalow, but in that short distance Gael from somewhere dredged up enough courage to turn and face him as soon as they got inside the house.

Her voice husky and trembling she said, 'I'm—I'm not going to be treated like this. It doesn't matter what you—

you think I've done, you have no right to take the law into your own hands and punish me like this.' She tried to steady her voice, her hands clutching at her evening bag. 'I know how terrible it was for you to lose your fiancée, to lose someone you love, but . . .'

His voice cut in scathingly, 'You'll never know!'

Gael stared at him for a moment and then said with quiet bitter sadness, 'Oh, but I do.'

The obviously deepfelt sincerity of her answer clearly surprised him, because his eyes widened and then drew together in a frown, but before he could speak Gael drew herself up and spoke with a quiet dignity that was far more compelling than anger or pleading. 'I know you hate me, but there's nothing I can do about that. Nothing is going to change what's happened between us. But I refuse to be bullied and threatened into doing what you want. And it's no good looking at me like that, because I mean it,' she added as his eyes narrowed dangerously. 'All right, you used brute force to frighten me into it tonight, but you can't go on forever saying that I'm recovering from a breakdown or something, because sooner or later people are going to start asking questions and wondering why. They might even start wondering whether you're the cause of my "illness". And you can't watch me all the time; even tonight I could have created a scene; poured wine over Norah Taylor or insulted Mark Ellis, for example. Okay, being you you'd probably have talked your way out of it— this time, but just how many times do you think you can get away with that kind of thing? And you can't lock me up in this house because then you'll be defeating your own object as well as making people suspicious—especially when you don't let me have any medical attention.' Her voice hardened. 'Whatever you say, whatever you do, I can still make you lose this job.'

Sneeringly he said silkily, 'Are you trying to threaten me?'

Hastily Gael disclaimed, 'No. No, I'm not.' She forced herself not to back away from this coiled-spring menace. Perhaps it was the drink that gave her Dutch courage, but somehow she managed to say steadily, 'But I am offering to make a bargain with you. If you want to keep this job then you'll need a hostess to welcome and look after all the new officials and their families when they come out here to work on the hospital project. How long do you think it will take before they all arrive?'

Slowly he answered, 'Most of them should be here within six months, I would think.'

'All right.' Gael's voice cracked a little but she went on doggedly. 'Then for my side of the bargain I'll agree to act as your—your hostess for six months and to undertake all the duties and entertaining that such a position entails.'

Silkily he asked, 'And in return?'

'And in return I expect you to treat me with the consideration you would show any other person with whom you work in close contact.' She took a deep breath. 'And I also expect you to let me leave here at the end of six months and for our—our marriage to be annulled. It can be done quietly in England so that no one here need know about it; and by then it will be the rainy season and you can tell people that I went home because I couldn't stand the climate or something.'

Leo's eyebrows rose mockingly. 'And do you really expect me to agree to your terms?'

'You don't have any choice. You've tried to cow me with

threats and to shatter my confidence by your betrayal, and you may have succeeded tonight, but you won't again. I'm as capable of carrying out my threats as you are, and I *will not* let you treat me like dirt! I'll give you six months of my time or I'll ruin you with your company.'

His face taut, Leo said grimly, 'Six months is hardly a just repayment for the debt you owe me.'

Gael's chin came up. 'I owe you nothing!' His eyes blazed suddenly and for a sickening moment she thought he was going to hit her, but instinct made her say with loathing in her voice, 'But if it's any comfort to you, then I can assure you that having to live in the same house as you for even six months will seem like a lifetime in hell!'

He drew a quick, hissing breath and then his face, his body slowly relaxed, and he gave her a strange, almost puzzled look. 'What a stubborn little fool you are! I hadn't realised there was any steel in your make-up.'

Gael hadn't known there was either, not until now, but she wasn't going to let him know that. 'You'll agree to the bargain, then?' she asked steadily, not letting her hope and fear sound in her voice.

Leo looked at her for a long moment, his expression unreadable, while Gael waited, her heart beating in anxious trepidation. If this didn't work . . .

'All right, I agree.'

She let out her breath on a great inner sigh of relief, but hurriedly pushed home her advantage. 'And there's one other thing—I'm not under any circumstances going to join the Country Club.'

To her surprise he hardly hesitated. 'Very well.' He looked at her keenly and then said in a quiet, deadly tone that sent shivers up her spine, 'But if you break your side

of the bargain, or stray from it by one iota, then you'll wish
you'd never been born. And just remember that if you start
by behaving as the perfect wife and hostess and then break
the bargain and try to carry out your threat, then everyone
will believe you're quite mad!'

For a few minutes they stood looking at one another,
each adjusting themself to the new arrangement. Then Leo
nodded, 'Just so long as we understand one another.'

Gael, too, nodded and then turned tiredly away, feeling
suddenly drained and weary, all her energy spent in the fight
for survival, for it was nothing less. At her door she glanced
back; Leo was still standing where she had left him, looking after her with an expression on his face which she had
never seen before and couldn't even begin to fathom.

If Gael expected any slackening in Leo's attitude towards
her after their agreement, then she was destined for disappointment. True, he made no attempt to hurt her or
threaten her physically again, but, if anything, his manner
seemed to harden and left her in no doubt that he still
despised her, treating her with a cold contempt that still
had the power to make her shrivel inside however much she
tried to fight it. But that was in private, of course. In public
he acted the attentive husband, calling her darling and putting a casually possessive arm round her waist or across her
shoulders in the age-old protective gesture of a man for his
woman. It had the desired effect; everyone thought that he
was devoted to her and admired him for it, but Gael found
it the hardest part of all to bear. His hypocrisy made her
feel physically ill and she would quickly move away from
his side, unable to bear the touch of his hand. People must
have noticed and their sympathy for Leo increased because
of it, but Gael couldn't help it, she just couldn't bear to be
close to him.

During the first few weeks, as the hospital project began to take off, several experts began to arrive with their families, and it was Gael's job to go in a company car to meet them at the airport and to escort them to the bungalow assigned to them, making sure they had everything they needed, that places had been reserved for their children in the school exclusively for Europeans in the area, and to invite them to a dinner party as soon as they had settled in so that they could meet other British people. Only a few of them were men who had been previously employed by the company on other projects, most of them were newly recruited especially for the two- to three-year period of this assignment and were completely unused to living abroad at all, let alone anywhere so far from home. So many of the wives looked to Gael for reassurance, often phoning to find out the simplest things that they could have learnt just from asking their servants, but often it was something more complicated, in which case, if Gael couldn't find out the answer, she referred them to Norah Taylor, who had lived in Bali for several years and who was, of course, only too happy to usurp Gael's role and make her out to be a moron.

At first having something constructive to do helped Gael to take her mind off her own problems, but as the first rush ended she found that time began to drag. When they entertained, all she had to do was to tell Pak Amat how many people were expected—which governed whether it was to be a sit-down meal or a buffet—and he and Kartini would do the rest, even down to arranging the flowers and putting out ashtrays. Gael had nothing to do but to dress herself in one of the many evening dresses she had brought with her, put up her fine blonde hair into a more sophisticated style, to greet Leo's guests with a false smile and then just to listen to them politely without allowing them to draw her out and satisfy their natural curiosity about her. And if they came to the conclusion that she was cold and withdrawn she couldn't help it; the only way she was going to survive these six months was by building a thick wall around herself and living inside it like a recluse, letting no one in or even to make a chink in the thick steel armour-plating of that wall.

The evenings alone with Leo were as hellish as she had imagined they would be. As soon as he came home Gael would go into her room and not come out until it was time for dinner. They would then eat in a stony silence almost as if the other person didn't exist, and then Gael would go back to her room to spend the rest of the evening reading, or writing to her sister and other friends back in England. At the weekends Leo simply went to the site office or else alone to the Country Club to play tennis or swim. During the day Gael would sunbathe in the garden, her fair skin tanning quickly in that everlasting sunshine. A couple of times she had tried sunbathing on the beach, but had been joined by other women neighbours who were sure she was lonely but too shy to ask for company, and had then proceeded to prattle on about babies, homes, husbands, until that lost, bitter feeling came back and Gael couldn't stand it any longer and had made an excuse and hurried back to the privacy of the garden, leaving the women extremely offended by her abruptness.

The arrival of her art things helped, but there are just so many objects you can paint or draw in one garden and she began to feel very restless, pacing up and down the garden as if it was a cage. As yet she had seen little of the island, only the estate and the road to and from the airport. She had no car to get round in, of course, and it was just too hot to go out walking for a long distance. The flowering hedges of the garden began to seem like prison walls as her frustration and boredom increased. But still she found no temptation to join the Country Club and go there almost every day as most of the other wives did; she was still too vulnerable, too much in a state of emotional shock to be able to act a part each and every day. It was bad enough when she had to appear in public with Leo, her nerves then were always mangled and stretched to breaking point and it would take her days to recover.

She began to get desperate, realising that if she didn't have some means of getting completely away from the bungalow for a while she might really break down. The beach was no good, there were always people there and she could feel their eyes on her, their tongues wagging about her, if she attempted to walk alone there. She supposed she could have asked Leo to let her have a company car so that she could go shopping in Denpasar, but pride held her back; not only would she have had to ask for the car but also for money to spend, and she wasn't going to give him the satisfaction of hearing her ask a favour. The servants did all the shopping in the local markets and Leo paid them direct, and anything else they needed was delivered and charged to accounts which Leo also settled, so Gael never handled any money. It was a deliberate policy, she supposed, designed to make her even more dependent on Leo, to make her life with him even more humiliating.

Her means of escape she discovered quite by chance. Often now, she awoke in the very early hours of the morning and was unable to go to sleep again, tossing and turning uncomfortably in the big bed. One day she couldn't stand it any longer and got up to get herself a cool drink. Silently she padded on bare feet out to the kitchen where she poured herself a glass of orange juice from the fridge, then she turned to go back to her room, but she paused as she saw the first signs of dawn breaking through the uncurtained windows. On impulse she pushed open the French doors and went out on to the veranda, curling herself up on one of the rattan chairs, her bare feet tucked under her as she sipped her drink and watched the blackness of night recede before the triumphant dawn of the new day.

For a while she lost herself in it, forgot everything except the wonder of the colours that filled her eyes, but then the sound of voices brought her sharply back to reality and she saw Pak Amat and Kartini turn into the driveway from the road. They were riding a bicycle, an ancient and rather rusty machine, with Pak Amat on the saddle and Kartini sitting sideways on a carrier at the back, a basket of groceries perched on her head and swaying precariously as they turned the corner. But it was the bicycle that riveted Gael's attention. If only she had a bicycle! She watched as the servants dismounted and unloaded another heavy basket strapped to the front, then they carefully and almost reverently wheeled the machine into a small storeroom attached to the garage; evidently bicycles were prized like Rolls-Royces in Bali.

Later that morning, immediately after she had heard Leo leave for the office, Gael went into the kitchen, determined to find out how she could get a bicycle. The servants were surprised at her request but told her that there was a place where they could be bought at the next village.

'Are they very expensive? Do they cost a lot?' she amended as she saw their puzzled faces.

They nodded and her heart sank, but when, after some

discussion, they named the number of rupiah it would need to buy a bicycle and she translated it into sterling, Gael realised that by Western standards it was quite a small amount.

She showed them a camera she had brought with her from England. 'Do you think you could sell this for me and use the money to buy a bicycle?' she asked anxiously.

Pak Amat took the camera from her and examined it. 'Yes, *njonya*, but I will have to take it to Denpasar. There is no one here who will buy.'

Eagerly Gael asked, 'Can you go today?'

'Yes, *njonya*, if that is your wish.'

He turned to go, but Gael put out a hand to stop him. 'Please— —' She hesitated, but it had to be said. 'Please, I don't want Tuan Kane to know about the bicycle.' She looked at them pleadingly, knowing that they must be wondering at her odd behaviour. But presumably they were used to odd requests, probably thought all Europeans strange, because they merely nodded and smiled, their faces breaking naturally into wide grins.

Gael was on fire with impatience until Pak Amat got back, which he did about four in the afternoon, triumphantly riding an old-fashioned upright bicycle, painted black and with a very large basket on the front. The saddle looked hard and uncomfortable and Gael was sure it would be a positive boneshaker, but even that couldn't detract from her excitement. Pak Amat and Kartini caught her mood and they all crowded round the bicycle, ringing the bell, trying the brakes, laughing and chattering.

'You see, is very good bicycle. You try it, *njonya*,' Pak Amat said, eager that she should see how well he had chosen for her.

Gingerly Gael got on and rode down the garden. For a few minutes she wobbled precariously; she hadn't ridden a bike since she was a schoolgirl, but soon her balance came back and she rode round and round the lawn, the servants running along either side of her, clapping their hands and shouting encouragement. Gael rang the strident-noted bell loudly and laughed. It was the first time she had laughed since she had arrived in Bali.

Afterwards they put the bicycle away in the little store room, no one saying anything but tacitly putting it behind some garden equipment, out of sight of anyone casually looking in.

That evening Gael noticed that she had a little colour in her cheeks and her eyes weren't as dull and lack-lustre as they had been. At last she could look forward to tomorrow instead of dreading it as something that had to be got through, the only compensation being that it was one day nearer the end of the six months and her freedom from Leo. At dinner she ate with more appetite than she had known for weeks, usually she was too tense to do more than pick at her food, but tonight she felt really hungry and spooned a second helping of savoury rice and noodles on to her plate. Glancing up, she saw Leo watching her.

'I'm glad to see you're eating properly,' he remarked. 'You're getting too thin.'

Gael returned his look coldly. 'Don't tell me you were worried about me?'

Leo shrugged. 'Not particularly. If you want to starve yourself, that's your own stupidity. I'm just glad you seem to be becoming adult enough to face up to reality at last, that's all.'

'The reality of having to live with a man who's a liar and

a cheat, do you mean?' she asked tauntingly.

His lips thinned. 'No, the reality of facing up to your own mistakes and accepting the punishment for them.'

Gael glared across the table at him. 'And just what gives you the right to inflict any punishment you see fit? I was tried and punished within the law. But the magistrates took everything into consideration; the ice on the road, the speed of the other car, whereas all you can think about is revenge.' She stood up, her meal forgotten. 'You're the one who's afraid of facing reality, of facing the fact that your fiancée is dead! Do you really think that hurting me is going to make any difference? She'll still be dead when you finally have to let me go, won't she? Nothing can change that! Nothing can bring her back!' She broke off abruptly and headed for the door.

Leo, his face very white, said curtly. 'Sit down.'

'Go to hell!'

He moved so swiftly that she hardly saw him, but even as her hand closed on the door knob, he pulled her round and sent her bumping against the wall. Catching hold of her wrists he pinned them against the wall, leaning his body against hers so that she couldn't struggle, his eyes, blazingly angry, only a few inches away.

'You want reality,' he said grimly. *'Well, this is it!* That trial in England means less than nothing. *This* is what matters. The fact that you're completely within my power, that I can use you any way I want. And we made a bargain, remember? But you've come damn near to breaking it tonight.' His tone became jeering. 'But perhaps you've decided that you like my company and want to stay on here with me, is that it? *Is that it?*' he repeated forcefully when she didn't answer.

'No!' Gael turned her head away. 'You know it isn't.'

'All right.' He took his weight off her and let go of her wrists. 'But just remember that the next time you feel like stepping out of line. Now go and finish your meal.'

Slowly Gael obeyed him, but her new-found appetite had disappeared completely, although Leo continued to eat as if nothing had happened. She gazed at him in miserable helplessness, the hurt as raw as ever. But then she remembered the bicycle and was overwhelmed by gratitude that it was there, waiting for her tomorrow. Tomorrow as soon as he had left the house she would ride out on it for a few hours of sheer escapism. But she mustn't ever let Leo find out that she had it, because she was quite certain he would take satisfaction in depriving her of it.

Calf muscles aching and out of breath, Gael reached the brow of the hill and stopped to rest for a minute, balancing the bicycle by putting one foot on the ground. She had been right about it being a boneshaker; her behind already felt bruised and she had an idea that it was going to be painful to sit down for quite some time. But it was well worth every bruise, every aching muscle. Looking around her, she felt her spirits lift enormously. Behind her there were the endless terraces of padi fields, to her right the Indian Ocean, and right in front of her a narrow road bordered by exotic shrubs and palm trees that dropped in a steep incline to a sprawling village. Gael took off her sunhat and stuffed it in the basket, got back on the bicycle and pedalled fast to the beginning of the slope, then took her feet off the pedals and freewheeled down the hill, her hair streaming out behind her, a laugh of sheer, almost childish delight on her lips.

Near the village several children saw her coming and fell in behind her, shouting and laughing. A couple of dogs came into sight chasing a squealing piglet and Gael rang her bell furiously. Immediately the dogs began to chase her instead, so that Gael came to a halt on the outskirts of the village in the centre of a noisy crowd of children and animals. The children were all dark-haired and dark-skinned but were neatly dressed in white shirts or blouses, the boys in shorts, the girls in short skirts, their hair drawn back from their faces. Most of them were barefoot, but some had brightly-coloured plastic flip-flops. But all of them, even to the tiny tot held in its big sister's arms, had great grins on their faces as they laughed at her, at themselves, at life. Gael remembered reading in her guide book that children on Bali are left very much to fend for themselves and are never smacked because it is believed it would harm their spirits; maybe that was why they all looked so happy.

She wandered through the village, stopping to gaze at the elaborately carved façade of a Hindu temple, of which there were many on this small island that had the largest Hindu population in the world. The ornate gates of the temple were very tall and flanked by huge stone figures of a fat, ugly god carrying a sword, and through the gates she could see steps leading up to the thatched roof temple, the whole of the front of the building covered with oriental carving in high relief. The village was criss-crossed by paths leading to groups of buildings surrounded by walls, which Gael guessed must be the family compounds or *kampung* in which most Balinese lived, often several generations of the family living in the same house. The buildings were very simple, just mud walls and thatched roofs, with a small family shrine where every day small palm-leaf baskets filled with flowers or rice were placed as offerings to the spirits of their ancestors. But rising noisily from each compound came the strident tones of transistors tuned to Radio Australia.

Women dressed in batik-dyed sarongs and over-blouses called *kebayas* made their way to the village market with impossibly high and heavy loads balanced on top of pads of cloth on their heads. One woman even had a heavy metal pot full of water on her head and hardly seemed aware of it as she strode rapidly along. The market was crowded with people, with goods for sale, and with dogs. There seemed to be dogs everywhere, darting in and out of the stalls and trying to steal from the huge woven baskets laden with vegetables, fish and gorgeous mouth-watering fruits. There were clothes, blankets, lengths of material, all in bright exciting colours, but most fascinating of all Gael found the spice stalls, their scents tantalising her nostrils, their colours and strange shapes delighting her eyes and making her long for an easel and paints.

A tourist bus from one of the coastal hotels had stopped in the village and now the guide collected up his flock and led them down a side road. Scenting something interesting, Gael picked up her bike and followed. Their destination was a stone carving school where young boys were being taught by a master sculptor to make mythological figures similar to the ones she had seen outside the temple. The stone was soft and had to be wetted before it could be carved, and often the boys had to stand on stools to reach figures that were taller than they were themselves. Gael found the carvings fascinating and would have loved to be able to buy one of the smaller ones as several of the tourists did, but instead she sat down unobtrusively in a corner and began to draw the fat demons, spirits and gods, then turned a page and began to sketch the workroom with the boys intent on their work.

The time flew by that day and for the first time she began to feel alive again, as if she had been in a state of deep shock and was only now starting to recover. Almost every day now, as soon as Leo left, Gael would collect a picnic lunch from Kartini and set off to explore, with a map filched from Leo's car as her guide. More often than not she ventured inland, there were too many new hotels and tourists along the coast, and she enjoyed trying to sketch the strange terraced ricefields, but one day when it was particularly hot, the sea beckoned and she found a narrow lane only a mile or so from the bungalow that she hadn't noticed before, and followed it down towards the shore.

It didn't lead directly to the sea, though, but to the crumbling gateway of what must once have been an imposing entrance to a large house. Curiously Gael walked a little way and saw an overgrown driveway, again going in the direction of the shore. It was very hot and she was reluctant to go all the way back up the lane to find another route, so with only a slight hesitation she went on up the driveway, sure that the place had long ago been deserted.

At the end of the drive there stood an old Dutch colonial-style plantation house, surprisingly intact, but heavily overgrown with flowering creeper which had hungrily climbed over the veranda and balconies which ran all round the building. It had once been painted white, but the paint had peeled long ago under the hot sun and now the woodwork was cracked and grey, and there were several tiles missing from the roof. The whole place looked neglected, as if a strong wind would make it collapse like a house of cards.

Gael stood in the sweep of the drive, holding her bicycle and gazing up at the empty windows. The house should have made her feel shivery, but it didn't; there was something warm and friendly about it, as if it lay slumbering in the sun, resting after a lifetime of giving comfort and shelter. Slowly she followed the path round the side of the house, trying to peer in at the windows, but they were too high for her. At the back of the house there was a terrace and what had once been a meticulously laid out garden but was now virtually a wilderness of exotic plants. Gael began to get excited. If the house was empty . . . She propped her bicycle against a tree and went up the wide steps leading to the veranda, treading carefully in case the boards were rotten, but they seemed sound and she crossed to peer in at the windows. But to her disappointment on closer inspection they proved to be shuttered from the inside on the whole of the ground floor, there wasn't even a chink where she could see in. The doors too, when she tentatively tried them, turned out to be securely locked.

Going down the steps into the garden again, Gael looked back wistfully at the house. Her sketchbook was rapidly becoming filled with scenes of native life and she longed to be able to transfer some of the drawings on to canvas, but she had only her bedroom to use as a studio and the light wasn't very good. Also she felt extremely reluctant to paint at the bungalow; there was too much tension in the air there for her ever to relax enough to work easily and well. And there was also the mind-bending possibility that Leo might see her work and pull that to shreds, destroy it as he had destroyed the rest of her life, and that was a risk she wasn't prepared to take. Her work was all she had left now and she was going to guard it like a child. For a while, on seeing the empty house, she had had a mad hope that she might be able to get in and perhaps use one of the upper rooms as a studio, but obviously someone still owned it and cared enough about it to keep it secure, so the idea was out of the question.

Gael sighed frustratedly, but then shrugged and went to get her bathing things from her bicycle basket. She found a stone path leading down to the sea and changed behind a palm tree, not that she need have bothered, for the cove, in which the house was roughly in the centre, was completely deserted, with only the sounds of the surf breaking and birds flying noisily through the trees to mar the hot stillness.

The sea felt deliciously cool and she swam about near the edge for quite some time; she wasn't a strong enough swimmer to venture out of her depth. From the sea she looked back along the shore to each end of the cove; the only signs of life were the walls of a house set high up on the promontory that formed the right-hand arm of the bay. It looked like a long, low building, but it was too far away for her to make out any details, and much too far away to detract from the rapid feeling of ownership that she was starting to have about the place.

Feeling hungry, she went back into the garden and spread her towel out on the grass of what had once been a lawn and began to eat her picnic lunch. The sun was beautifully hot and she began to feel the sense of well-being that only seems to come when lying in the sun with absolutely nothing to do. She undid the halter fastening of her bikini top so that she wouldn't have white marks, then thought, What the hell? There's no one to see, and feeling greatly daring took the top off altogether and dropped it in the grass beside her. The sun was like a caress on her bare breasts and she moved sensuously, understanding why so many girls on the Continent went topless. Picking up her sunhat, she perched it on the front of her head, so that it covered her eyes, and quietly drifted off to sleep.

Her hat must have fallen off because the sun was in her eyes and she stirred a little, but then the sun was blotted out again by a dark shadow. Something soft brushed her lips and then became harder and she realised she was being kissed. Dreamily she murmured, 'Leo' and opened her mouth as the kiss became more demanding.

And then suddenly she was completely awake. She opened her eyes and gave a cry of alarm as she pushed herself away from the man bending over her.

In no way put out, he grinned down at her and said, 'Hallo, sleeping beauty.'

CHAPTER FIVE

GAEL gazed in consternation as the man, a complete stranger, looked her over appreciatively. Then she realised where his eyes had settled and hastily grabbed her towel and wrapped it round her.

'Who are you?' she demanded furiously.

The man grinned again. 'Prince Charming, of course. Who else?'

He had a definite Australian accent and was dressed in

casual clothes; a shirt open to the waist to reveal a hairy chest, and pale blue shorts. He looked very big and tough, with muscular shoulders and legs like tree-trunks. He was quite good-looking in a craggy kind of way and his skin was tanned a deep brown so it was difficult to tell his age, but there were tell-tale flecks of grey at the sides of his thick brown hair that made Gael think that he must be older than he first appeared to be.

She reached out for her bikini top, but the man picked it up first. For a moment he held it, dangling it in his fingers. Gael's eyes met his and showed fear, all too well aware that she was alone and vulnerable, but he merely tossed the top to her.

'Here. Although it's a crime to cover them up.' He turned so that he sat with his back to her while she put the top on, her fingers fumbling with the fastening.

He turned round again as she stood up and began to hastily collect the bits and pieces from her picnic.

'Don't run away yet. Here, I brought you a beer,' he offered.

Gael looked at him and hesitated. She wasn't afraid any more. Somehow, despite the fact that he had kissed her awake, she knew that he wouldn't harm her. If he had been going to he wouldn't have let her dress. Slowly she sat down on the grass again.

'You knew I was here?'

He pulled the ring off a beer can and handed it to her. 'Sure, I saw you swimming in the bay.'

'I didn't see anyone.'

'You wouldn't—I was on the terrace of my house. Up yonder.' He gestured towards the right arm of the bay.

'You live in that house on the headland?'

'That's right.'

He took a swig of his beer and Gael remembered her own. It tasted bitter to her palate but was infinitely cool and refreshing.

'Mm. How did you manage to keep it so cool?' she asked.

'I keep a few down here for when I come swimming.' He glanced at her bike. 'You come far?'

Immediately a shutter came down over Gael's face. 'No, not far,' she answered shortly.

'Strange I haven't seen you around before.' His eyes glanced at her casually when she didn't answer, but Gael had the feeling that he saw a great deal. 'My name's Dirk Vanderman, by the way.'

'That sounds Dutch,' she commented.

'It's of Dutch descent. But I've lived most of my life in Australia.'

Gael smiled slightly. 'I've noticed.'

He grinned and lay back in the grass, his head resting on his arms. 'But Bali's the place. Bali's the best place in the world.'

'You sound very partisan,' Gael observed.

'Why not? I was born here, and my family lived here for generations. Do you like it?'

'Oh, yes, very much,' Gael said enthusiastically. 'I've only really just started to get to know it. But it's so alive, so full of colour.'

'You're not a tourist, then?'

'No!' Gael said shortly. Then more calmly, 'No, I live here.' She sipped her beer for a moment before saying tentatively, 'You say you live nearby, then perhaps you know about this house? Why no one lives here?'

He turned on to his stomach and looked at her for a moment, then at the house. 'It's been empty for some years, the present owner finds it too big and old-fashioned. It would need a fortune spent on it to modernise it and get it fit to live in again.'

'But it would be a shame to let the house just fall to pieces,' Gael exclaimed.

Confidently he replied, 'Oh, I don't think he'd let it do that.'

'Do you know the house?' she asked.

'Yes, very well. I keep an eye on it for the owner—that's why I came down. When I saw you bathing I thought you might be one of a party of young people who might do some damage to it.'

Gael looked at him in sudden excitement. 'Do you—do you have a key?'

He didn't look at her, but at the house. 'Why so interested?'

She shrugged rather helplessly. 'I don't know. There's just something about the place. It looks as if it's ready to wake up and be lived in again. As if it's got tired of waiting.'

Dirk Vanderman stood up and reached down a hand to her. 'Come on, the door's already open. Where do you think I got the beer?'

The house was beautiful, and in a much better state of preservation than Gael had expected. Dirk threw open the shutters to reveal large high-ceilinged rooms full of good antique furniture, rather heavy Dutch pieces, of course, but they fitted in perfectly with the house. Most of the furniture lay under dust sheets, but it was obvious that the place was cleaned regularly because the layer of dust was very thin and there were no cobwebs hanging down to make it spooky. A wide, exquisitely carved staircase climbed in a semi-circle up to the galleried landing on the first floor, and from this opened off large sunny bedrooms, most of them empty now, but a few still fitted out with furniture.

Gael went happily from room to room, exclaiming with delight and listening with interest to the stories Dirk told her about the family that had lived there. He seemed to know a great deal about them and once, in the children's nursery, he pushed an old rocking horse with his foot, a reminiscent look on his face which quickly changed to his usual grin when he saw that Gael was watching him. But it was one of the empty bedrooms at the back of the house that drew Gael's biggest sigh of envy.

Dirk opened the shutters and the room filled with light, the clear light from the sea. 'Oh, this would be perfect. Just perfect!'

His eyebrows rose in surprise. 'Perfect for what?'

'Oh, it doesn't matter.' She tried to shrug it off. 'It was just a wild idea I had.'

'So tell me. What idea?'

Reluctantly she answered. 'Well, you see I paint a little. But where I'm—I'm living at the moment there isn't enough space, and the light's wrong. And I thought—well, that this would make a perfect studio.'

Dirk frowned and she turned away. 'I said it was a wild idea,' she added with a harsh laugh, angry that she had even voiced her desire.

But he put out a hand to stop her as she went to walk quickly out of the door. 'Don't be so damn touchy. You say you just want to use it to paint?'

'Yes.' Gael waited, hope rising again.

'How often would you want to come here?'

'I don't know. I hadn't thought about it. Only during the week, not at weekends.'

'No.' He glanced down and Gael followed his eyes to realise with a sick feeling that he was looking at her wedding ring. 'Are you sure that your—family would approve of your coming here?'

Gael stiffened, her eyes bleak. 'I don't need anyone's approval. But I,' she paused and looked at him pleadingly, 'but I *do* need somewhere to paint.'

Dirk looked at her consideringly, then nodded. 'Okay, you can have the use of this room. I'll get a key to the front door cut for you so that you can come and go when you please. If you come here tomorrow morning I'll give it to you.'

'Oh, Dirk, that's wonderful! Thank you—thank you so much. You don't know how much this means to me. May I bring some of my things tomorrow?'

She turned a happy, excited face up to him, eyes sparkling like sapphires, cheeks flushed. An arrested look came into Dirk's face, but as Gael continued to look at him expectantly he gave a curious sort of jerk and then said, 'Sure, bring whatever you want. But I think it would be better if you didn't tell anyone that I'm letting you use the place. Other people might try to turn it into an artists' colony or something. And then the owner might get to hear about it,' he added as an afterthought.

'Oh, no, I won't tell a soul,' Gael assured him fervently. The last thing she wanted was for anyone to find out; they might tell Leo.

She took another look through the windows at the view over the sea, promising herself that that was the first thing she would paint. The shadows were longer than she expected, the sun further over in the sky. Hastily she looked at her watch. 'Oh, no! Look at the time. If I don't rush I shall be late and ...' She broke off abruptly. She had been going to say, And Leo will be home, but she didn't want Dirk to know about Leo, she wanted the two parts of her life to be completely separate. Turning to Dirk, she spoke quickly to cover her slip.

'I must fly, I'm sorry. Thank you for showing me over the house, thank you for saying I can come and paint here. I'll see you tomorrow.'

She turned and ran round the gallery and started down the staircase. Dirk followed her more slowly and leant on the banister of the gallery. 'Hey!' he called as she was half-way down.

Gael stopped and looked up at him, the curve in the stairs bringing her almost opposite him.

'You haven't told me your name.'

For a moment she thought of lying to him, of hiding behind an alias, but then she called back, 'It's Gael.'

'Just Gael?'

Emphatically she said, 'Just Gael,' and ran down the rest of the stairs.

In the excitement of the day she had forgotten that they were entertaining some new arrivals that evening and that Leo would be home early, so she had to pedal furiously back to the bungalow. She just made it in time to hide her bicycle and was actually running through the French windows as Leo turned into the driveway. He grabbed the bathroom first and so she was ready only just before the first couple arrived. She emerged from her room, still trying to do up a bracelet, and Leo ran his eyes over her as he always did, checking that she looked the part, she supposed.

'Here, let me do that up for you,' and he reached out to take her arm.

For a moment she hesitated, reluctant to have him touch her, then held out her wrist.

'What took you so long?' he asked.

His touch sent electric shocks along her skin and she had to force herself to hold her hand steady. 'What? Oh, I was busy.'

He looked at her sharply, not letting go of her hand. 'Busy? Doing what?'

Panic seized her as she tried to think of a convincing lie, but mercifully their first guests arrived and she was able to avoid answering.

For the first time she enjoyed the dinner party, was able to relax and chat easily, and even take pleasure in the meal and the way it was served. There were eight people, so she was some way from Leo, which helped, of course, and when they moved back into the sitting-room for coffee she took care to sit as far away from him as possible.

One of their guests was Dr Tom Stanton and he nodded at her approvingly. 'You're looking a whole lot better than you did when you came here. I quite expected to have you as a patient, but you seem to have picked up tremendously this last week or so.'

Gael smiled at him, but was surprised that he had been keeping such a close eye on her. She had met him quite often because she always made a point of introducing all the new arrivals to him when she took them to see the hospital as part of the normal round of showing them the area.

Lightly she said, 'Oh, that's just because I've got a tan now. Everyone looks pale and unhealthy when they first come out from England.'

His kindly eyes frowned at her. 'Yes, but they don't all look as if they were on the edge of a nervous breakdown,' he said bluntly. 'Still, I'm glad you seem to have sorted yourself out, but if you do need any help you know where to find me.' He nodded, and without waiting for her to speak, got up and looked round the room for his wife. 'I'm afraid we must be going—I've got a very pregnant patient who's bound to have her baby in the middle of the night. They nearly always do,' he added with a chuckle.

Their going broke the party up and Leo and Gael stood at the top of the steps to wave them on their way. When they had gone, Gael immediately turned to go in, but Leo stopped her.

'Just a moment, I want to talk to you. Let's take a stroll round the garden, shall we?'

Reluctantly Gael said, 'Very well,' and went down the steps and along the path at the side of the house round to the back. The scent of flowers came gently on the breeze. It was a perfect tropical night, the sky like black velvet scattered with diamonds. Gael looked up at the sky and tried to make out the patterns of the stars, but the constellations in this hemisphere were completely strange to her. I shall have to get a book about astronomy, she thought idly as she reached up to break off a piece of white-flowered jasmine and drink in its spicy perfume.

Leo was standing a few feet away, smoking a cigarette, and when Gael turned she saw that he was watching her.

'You seem different tonight,' he said slowly.

'Do I?' She turned and began to walk on down the garden. They came to the gate and Leo opened it so that they could walk down to the beach.

'Yes. You seemed as if you were beginning to enjoy life again.'

Gael looked at him warily, afraid that he might take her newly-won freedom away from her. 'So what if I am? Did you really think I would go on'—she sought for a word— 'go on hurting because of what you did to me for ever? Well, maybe that doesn't suit you, maybe you would prefer me to be miserable and unhappy all the time. But I've got news for you, Leo Kane; people do get over things that hurt them. They learn to live with it and not live in the past. Well, I've done that even if you haven't. You can go on grieving for your girl-friend, and feeding your grief by hating me, if that's what you want.' She paused and then said clearly, 'But I've got over you now. There's nothing you can do to me that will ever hurt me again.'

She didn't quite know how he would react to her outburst, with his usual anger, she supposed, but she certainly didn't expect him to look at her for a long moment and then say slowly, 'I never realised just how much you would be hurt.'

Anger came to her then and she said sharply, 'Just what the hell did you expect?'

He shrugged. 'I don't know. I didn't think about it very much. All I could think of was finding you and getting you here—and I didn't care about how I did it.'

They had come to a stop at the edge of the sand. Above them the palm trees swayed gently, the breeze making sighing noises in the leaves, almost like soft singing, while the sound of the surf receded gently on the ebb tide, leaving the long stretch of wet sand glistening in the moonlight. But they were both oblivious to their surroundings as they faced each other in the moving shadows of the palms.

It was the first time Leo had ever talked to her like this and Gael wasn't sure how to take it. His anger seemed to have died, and she wondered if in fact he was at last starting to get over his fiancée's death. Maybe the revenge he had taken out on her had worked, had served to assuage his grief in some crazy kind of way, Gael thought bitterly. Well, bully for him! But if he thought that they could now drop the enmity between them, he was mistaken. Her feelings about him were too intense to be anything but highly emotional. It had to be love or hate, there could never be indifference. And he had killed her love once and for all and so she intended to go on hating him with every fibre of her being. Because only by hating him could she hope to get through these six months of proximity.

Slowly, feeling her way, she said, 'Well, you got what you wanted. You've got me here, doing what you want. You should feel very satisfied.'

He threw down his cigarette and ground it out under his heel. 'Yes, I suppose I should,' he said abruptly. He put his hands in his trouser pockets and walked on a few yards, then swung round to face her. 'There's a big celebration dinner and dance at the Club in a couple of weeks. It's their annual binge after the election of the new chairman and committee. I'd like to take you along.'

'You're ordering me to go, you mean,' Gael answered coldly. 'Why is it so important?'

'I've been elected to the committee—and all right, it would look odd if I went alone, but I'm asking you to come with me.'

'Why?' Gael asked derisively. 'So that the whole Club can see what an attentive and devoted husband you are? So that they can all feel even sorrier for you being married to such a social misfit?'

Leo's dark brows drew together into a frown. 'I want you to come as my wife,' he said grimly.

She laughed mirthlessly. 'Your wife? You must be joking! I'm not your wife, I'm just the poor fool who fell for your all too obvious charms. The dupe you're using to take your vengeance out on and to further your career.' Her mouth drew into a bitter line. 'All right, I'll go to the Club with you, because that's part of the bargain I made, but don't let's have any false ideas about what terms I go under. I do it on sufferance, for no other reason.'

He took his hands from his pockets and she saw they were balled into tight fists. 'It doesn't have to be that way, Gael. Not any more.'

She stared at him. The shadows played tricks and moved across his face so that she couldn't read his expression. 'Yes, it does,' she said heavily. 'There'll never be any other way.' Then she turned and ran through the flower-scented night back to the house.

Gael walked all the way to the plantation house the next morning, pushing the bicycle on which was strapped her easel and several canvases. The basket too was bulging with equipment so that she was panting with exertion by the time she got there.

Dirk was waiting for her, sitting on the steps of the back veranda and drinking a beer. Gael propped the bike against the rails and flopped down beside him, her breathing uneven. Without a word Dirk got up to fetch her a can of beer, not speaking until she had had a long drink and her breathing was steady again.

'You're a young fool, you know that? You could kill yourself lugging a load like that about in this heat when you're not used to it,' he admonished her. 'If you were my responsibility I'd have you over my knee and give you a good spanking!'

Gael grinned at him, completely at ease with him now. 'But I'm not your responsibility, am I?'

'No, more's the pity.' He stood up. 'Come on, let's get your stuff up to your room.'

'Studio,' Gael corrected him happily. 'That's what professional artists call their workrooms.'

Dirk helped her unpack the bike and carry the things upstairs, and Gael gave a gasp of pleasure when she walked into the room. It had been swept clean of dust, the windows polished, the paintwork washed until it shone. She put down the things she was carrying and turned to him in wonder.

'You cleaned it! You cleaned it out for me.'

He smiled. 'Well, I couldn't have you accusing me of being a lousy caretaker.' His expression changed and he put his hands on her shoulders. 'Hey, you're not crying, are you?'

'No. No, of course not.' Gael put up a finger to wipe away the sudden tears. 'It's just that—that no one's been so kind to me for a long time.'

His fingers tightened on her shoulders for a moment, then he said gruffly, 'It was nothing.' But in quite a different tone he said, 'Here, you're not one of those women who turn on the waterworks all the time, are you? Because if you are ...'

Gael laughed and disclaimed, 'No, of course not. I promise you it was only a temporary aberration.' Her voice softened. 'But thanks all the same.'

They brought up the rest of her things and then Dirk showed her an old table that he had thought she might like to use as a workbench and between them they carried it up the stairs, although Dirk was so strong that he took all the weight from the bottom and she merely had to keep the top legs clear of the stairs.

'There.' Dirk stood back and looked at the room. 'It's getting to look like a studio already. Is there anything else you need?'

'No, not at the moment, thanks.' She paused and then said rather awkwardly, 'Dirk, I—I know I should have asked you yesterday, but about the rent for the room. I'm afraid I don't have much money at the moment, but I can probably get some quite soon if you'll tell me how much you want,' she added, having already worked out what she could get Pak Amat to sell for her.

Dirk frowned. 'I don't want any rent, I'm glad to let you use it.'

Gael drew herself up a little. 'That's very kind of you and I really appreciate it, but I really would rather pay some rent. Make it a business arrangement rather than a favour.' She looked at him anxiously, hoping that he'd understand.

Luckily he did. He crossed to the table and opened her sketchbook, flicking over the pages, then he turned to her. 'Okay. How long would it take you to do a painting from one of these sketches?'

Gael shrugged. 'Oh, I don't know, two or three days perhaps. A week at the most.'

'Then I'll charge you one painting per calendar month, and that includes four cans of beer a day. Deal?'

She gurgled with laughter. 'It's a deal.'

'Right. Then let's go and have a beer now. Shifting that table has made me thirsty.'

They went outside again and shared the picnic lunch Gael had brought with her.

'You know, I think I might even bring my stuff over and

work on it here,' Dirk remarked. 'We'll be able to work in creative harmony,' he added with a touch of wry self-derision.

'What do you do, then?'

'I keep body and soul together by punching out a few feature articles on the typewriter.' His eyebrows rose mockingly when he saw her look of surprise. 'What's the matter? Do you think ignorant Colonials don't know how to write?'

'Of course not,' Gael exclaimed hastily. 'It's just that—well, that you look too *big* to be a writer!'

Dirk's eyes flew wide in astonishment, Gael realised the inanity of her remark, and then they both burst into laughter.

'Of all the bird-brained things to say—and typically female,' Dirk chuckled. But his eyes grew warm as he added, 'You know something? I think I'm going to enjoy having you around.'

Impulsively Gael put her hand out to cover his. 'Thanks, Dirk. I really appreciate it.'

'Any time.' He reached out with his other hand and lightly touched the ring on her finger. 'And any time you feel that you want to talk about that, or anything else—well, my shoulders are pretty broad.'

Gael took her hand away and covered it with her right one, as if to hide all reminders of that other life. 'I noticed,' she said unevenly.

Dirk pushed himself to his feet. 'I'll be getting along.' He tossed a key into her lap. 'Don't forget to lock up securely before you leave. So long.' And with a casual nod he walked away towards the beach.

Gael saw him often after that first day and gradually their time together evolved into a pleasant pattern. Dirk would set up a garden table in the shade of one of the trees on the edge of the lawn and tap away on his typewriter, while Gael took her easel out on to the balcony of her workroom and painted the view down to the sea. They would work contentedly in the peace of the morning until Dirk gave her a whistle and she joined him on the veranda for their first beer, then back to work until they had a longer break for a swim and then the lunch that Gael had brought, a much larger one now since she had told a surprised Pak Amat to pack twice as much. During this time they talked a lot; about art and books and places, a hundred abstract subjects, until after a while Dirk fell silent and, in the Balinese custom, took a siesta for a couple of hours. Sometimes Gael joined him, lying in the lush grass, but more often she went back to do more work on the current painting, working out the frustration of the long weeks when she had itched to have a brush in her hand.

Apart from that very first kiss, which Gael was sure he had given her only out of sheer devilment, because he just couldn't resist the impulse, Dirk always treated her with a casual friendliness that she found almost as therapeutic as her painting. Gradually her frozen heart began to thaw a little. Because Dirk was so much older than she, older than Leo even, she tended to think of him as, not a father-figure exactly, but perhaps as an uncle, one with whom she was on very good terms, who laughed at her and wasn't afraid to say what he thought, whether in criticism or praise. He was in fact just what she needed to start to restore her shattered confidence, to give her the sort of friendship that carried no ties and made no demands on her. That, and her workroom, provided a safe haven which she could run to, physically during her free days, and in her imagination

when she was forced to stay at the bungalow or go to some
social function with Leo.

But she would have to be careful; several times now she
had been miles away, deep in thought about scenes and
colours, or laughing inwardly at a remembered joke of
Dirk's, a smile of reminiscence on her lips, when she had
come back to reality to find Leo watching her narrowly, a
frown between his brows. Flames of panic had seized her
then; she mustn't let him suspect, mustn't let him even begin to think that she might have a life apart from the
bungalow. If she lost it now ... But that was too dreadful
even to contemplate.

To try to lull any suspicions he might have, Gael made
more of an effort to be sociable in public and when the
night of the dinner and dance at the Country Club came
round took extra care with her appearance, putting on a
long, deep-peach-coloured dress with a halter neck and
very low back that looked superb with her tan. Her hair
she swept up and back at the sides and fastened with clips
decorated with diamanté butterflies.

Leo was waiting for her in the sitting-room and she
stood, a thin smile on her lips as she waited for him to look
her over.

'Well, will I do for your precious Country Club?' she
asked scathingly. 'Good enough to attend the social occa-
sion of the year?'

Picking up a drink, he carried it over and handed it to
her. He stood looking down at her, his expression enig-
matic, then he said slowly, 'You look—very young.'

And make of that what she might, Gael thought in surprise. He moved away to get his own drink, tall, and
damnably good-looking in evening dress, but his face hard

and determined even in profile. He caught her watching him and Gael turned quickly away, her heart giving a sudden lurch. Oh God, let this hell soon be over!

But all during the drive to the Club, as they sat in a silence broken only by the noise of the engine and music on the radio, she thought about his comment on her youth. Bitterly she realised that she must always have seemed very juvenile and gauche to him, that he would never have even looked at someone so naïve if he hadn't deliberately sought her out for his own reasons. She gave a twisted cynical smile; perhaps if she hadn't been so naïve she might have seen through his false attentions and none of this would have happened, she would still have been at home. If only ... but those were the most useless words in the language. Gael recalled that Julia Symons, his dead fiancée, had been twenty-eight when she died, a sophisticated woman of the world who would have known how to take her place beside an up-and-coming business executive. No wonder Leo found her so unsophisticated in comparison!

Norah and Malcolm Taylor were waiting to meet them in the entrance of the Club.

'Leo, darling,' Norah gushed, 'how lovely to see you!' She glanced at Gael and gave her a patronising smile. 'And you've managed to persuade Gael to come with you. My, we *are* honoured, aren't we?'

She covered the sarcasm with a trill of laughter, but Gael was left in no doubt that Norah would take every opportunity that offered to make digs and snide remarks and do her best to spoil the evening for her. If she only knew, Gael thought with irony; nothing Norah could do could possibly make an evening spent in Leo's close company anything worse than the living hell it already was.

It wasn't so bad during dinner because Leo was seated opposite her and she could ignore him and concentrate on talking to the men on either side of her, but afterwards, when the room had been cleared for dancing and tables set round the edge of the floor, she had no choice but to sit next to him at the table reserved for them with the Taylors and other committee members and their respective spouses. Everyone was drinking freely, the room noisy with music and laughter as couples got up to dance. Norah and Malcolm took to the floor with some others from their table while the rest continued their conversations. Leo danced with Norah next and Gael dutifully got up to partner Malcolm, and after that one of the men she had sat next to at dinner.

Everyone sat down and chatted for a while, then one of the white-jacketed waiters brought another round of drinks. Gael took a long drink of hers; even though the room was air-conditioned it was still very hot. The band switched to a slow, haunting melody that had been very big in England when she had first started dating Leo. Her thoughts went unbidden back to that time and she gazed unseeingly down at the table.

'Let's dance, shall we?'

She felt Leo touch her arm and turned to find him looking at her expectantly. Her face filled with hatred and she jerked her arm away, the memories of the past leaving her raw and bleeding. 'No!' she spat at him, her voice thick with revulsion.

His eyes blazed in his suddenly taut face, but then he smiled, but the smile didn't reach his eyes. Leaning forward, he put his right arm round her waist and his left hand on her wrist.

'We made a bargain, remember?' he said silkily, his mouth close to her ear. 'If you want to break it, it's up to you. But you can be quite sure that I'll make you live to regret it during those long years you'll be with me!'

His voice had been filled with threatened menace, but from the way a woman across the table smiled at them indulgently, Gael realised that to everyone else it probably looked as if he was nibbling her ear!

'All right, I'll dance! Damn you!'

'Good. I was sure you'd see it my way.' He stood up, lifting her to her feet with him, his arm still round her waist, and he kept it there as he led her to the floor.

Gael stood stiffly, trying to hold herself away from him, but he pulled her close against him, his eyes looking down at her sardonically as she lost the silent struggle.

Leo held her so close that she could feel his body pressing hard against her own, smell the tanginess of his after-shave. From somewhere deep within her she felt a crying, aching need that was followed by a wave of sensuality that was so strong it made her shudder violently. Leo's arm tightened around her to prevent her trying to struggle again, but Gael couldn't have fought him now if she'd wanted to.

She had never danced with him before; all the time they had been dating he had never once taken her to a place where they could dance. She had thought then that it was because he didn't dance, but it was only now that the bitter truth hurt her. She lifted her head to look into his face so close to her own.

'Did she dance? Your fiancée?' she asked, her voice harsh with bitterness.

Leo swore under his breath. 'She has nothing to do with this,' he answered curtly.

'Doesn't she?' The hurt was too deep for Gael to care that she was heading into danger. 'Oh, but I think she does. It was because of her that you never took me dancing, wasn't it? Because you couldn't trust yourself to hold me in your arms for any length of time and not let your revulsion show on your face. My God, how you must have had to force yourself to touch me! How you must have cringed inside when you had to kiss me. But then, even someone as stupid and simple as I was unlikely to believe that a man loved her when he couldn't even bring himself to kiss her!'

Her voice had risen, but Leo said loudly, drowning her out, 'Yes, of course, darling, it is terribly hot. Let's get some air, shall we?' And taking her wrist in a vice-like grip he led her through some doors leading into the gardens.

Once out of earshot of the building he yanked her round to face him. 'You little fool! You agreed not to pick a fight in public.'

'I can't help it! I can't stand having to play a part in this farce of a marriage any longer. I can't stand having to live with you when I know that you hate me, that you can't even bear the sight of me. That you're wishing all the time that I was dead and *she* was alive!' She put her balled fists up to her head and banged them against her temples.

'Stop it!' Leo caught her wrists and pulled them down. Roughly he said, 'Can't you see that thinking about the past is only going to make the situation worse for you? You've just got to forget it and ...'

'Forget it?' Gael stared at him unbelievingly. 'Forget the way you lied and deceived me? Well, I don't even want to forget it. I just want you to let me go. To stop having to

live a lie and to be freed from this travesty we're living.'
She was almost shouting, her voice rising in near-hysteria.

'Shut up!' Leo pulled her roughly against him, his eyes
dark with anger. 'Shut up, do you hear me? If you get
hysterical I'll have to hit you.'

'Sadist!' she shot at him.

Through gritted teeth, Leo said, 'We are going back in
there and we are going to dance together until the music
ends, when we will go back to our table and smile and look
as if we're having a wonderful time. Do you understand?
Do you?'

Suddenly all the fight seemed to go out of her and her
shoulders sagged. Weakly she agreed, 'Yes, all right.'

They went back inside and stood at the edge of the floor
for a moment, waiting for a space in the crowded throng of
dancers. Gael looked over Leo's shoulders and saw that a
man had followed them in from the garden. There was
something about the powerful set of his shoulders that
looked vaguely familiar and then she saw that he was watching her intently. Her eyes met his, and with a shock that
was like jumping into an ice-cold pool she realised it was
Dirk!

CHAPTER SIX

As Gael put her hand into the pocket of her shorts, it
closed over the key to the plantation house. She sat astride
the bicycle, her feet resting on the ground, under the shade
of a huge banyan tree that grew on the edge of the lane that

led to the house. She had been sitting there for some time, trying to make up her mind to go down the driveway which was about fifty yards further along the lane. For the rest of the evening at the Country Club she had been sick with fear that Dirk would come across to her and she would have to introduce him to Leo, but they had joined the dancing before he could move to speak to her and then she had seen him go towards the bar. She had sat there in a state of nail-biting tension for another hour before they left, then she caught another glimpse of Dirk talking with some other men as she passed the bar to go to the cloakroom. She wasn't sure whether he noticed her because she deliberately turned her head and hurried away. And fortunately Leo had put her tenseness down to their recent row. It wasn't until they got back to the bungalow that it occurred to her that if Dirk had been out in the garden he might easily have overheard some, if not all, of their fight!

Which was why she hadn't been to her studio for two days, why she was still sitting here trying to make up her mind to go to the house and face Dirk. If he had heard, how would he react? Would he feel sorry for her? Want to know the whole story? Her mind cringed from both possibilities. No way could she bring herself to tell anyone of her humiliation at Leo's hands. And she couldn't stand pity. Sympathy perhaps—just. But never pity. The key was hot in her hand as she turned it over and over, trying to make up her mind. She thought of dropping it on the ground, letting the way it fell decide whether she would ever go to the house again, but then told herself she was a fool; she wasn't so far gone that she was going to let chance rule her life, was she? With a kick, she set the bicycle going and pedalled fast down the lane and into the avenue leading to the house before she could change her mind.

The sense of anticlimax when she found that Dirk wasn't there made her feel slightly ridiculous. She let herself in and took great comfort in the familiar surroundings of her workroom, throwing open the shutters to let the sun flood in and running her fingers lovingly, hungrily, over her canvases and brushes. She carried her easel out on to the balcony, set a new canvas on it and was soon contentedly transferring one of her sketches of village life to the larger framework.

She wore only a black bikini, her skin now so deeply tanned that she could stand out in even the hottest hours of the day. Her hair she had plaited into a long pigtail, and that, too, had been bleached into a lighter shade of gold by the sun. Absorbed in her work, she lost all track of time as the picture of a native market took shape.

A loud whistle from the garden below broke her concentration abruptly and made her jump. Dirk was standing in the garden looking up at her, hands on hips and dressed only in his usual frayed and faded denim shorts. He looked as strong as a tree.

'You coming for a swim before lunch?' he called up to her.

Gael hesitated, then shouted, 'Okay, be with you in a minute.' She carefully covered up the smudge she had made on the canvas when he had startled her, then grabbed the beach towel she kept there and ran down to join him.

He was already in the water and swimming strongly out to some rocks that jutted out into the sea below the promontory on which his villa stood. His powerful arms cut the sea cleanly, carrying him along in a fast, even crawl. Gael didn't even attempt anything so ambitious, her swimming was much better now than when she had arrived in Bali, but she had never yet managed to reach the rocks. Dirk would sit and watch her while she got as far as she could and when she turned to go back he would dive into the water again and quickly catch her up and stay beside her until they reached the shallows. But today Gael felt a sudden determination to reach the rocks and she struggled on with her schoolgirl breaststroke, slowly narrowing the gap. Her arms began to tire and she had to rest for a minute. Dirk was half lying on one of the largest of the rocks, watching her but making no move to help or encourage her. Until she saw him, she had been on the point of giving up and going back, but the look in his eyes was a definite challenge and she began to swim again, pushing her tired arms through water that seemed to press against her like something solid and heavy.

At last she reached the rocks and Dirk leaned down to bodily lift her up beside him. For several minutes she lay there panting for breath, completely spent.

'I—did it!' she gasped triumphantly.

He grinned. 'Sure you did. You can do anything if you want it badly enough.'

Gael lifted herself on one elbow and looked at him. 'The only thing is—I don't think I'll be able to get back!'

Dirk burst out laughing and reached out to pull her pigtail. 'You're one crazy female, do you know that?'

They lay there in silence for some time while Gael rested. If he's going to say anything about seeing me at the dance, he'll say it now, she thought, but as the silence lengthened and he lay, his head on his arms, eyes closed against the sun, she gradually began to relax. Perhaps he hadn't even recognised her.

Halfway back to the shore her strength gave out and he made her turn on her back while he towed her in, then put his arm round her and helped her to wade through the shallows to the sand. But it didn't matter; today she had reached the rocks and tomorrow she would do better, until eventually she would be able to do it alone. It was rather like the time she had to spend with Leo; the worst part was over and she only had to go on from day to day and eventually it would come to an end. She had been here nearly two months already, only four more to go!

'A penny for them.'

Dirk's voice interrupted her and she turned to smile at him. 'Oh, they're not for sale at any price.'

They went back into the garden to eat their lunch and Dirk started to tell her about the various art forms for which the Balinese were famous, how a certain area could concentrate on one form of art while the people in the next village were expert at something entirely different. He told her that the best wood-carvers and silversmiths in Indonesia were to be found on the island and mentioned the stone carvers that she had already seen at Batu Bulan.

'They catch them young here,' he said. 'They start teaching them batik—you know, the waxing and dyeing method of patterning cloth—almost before they can walk, and there's even a Batik Research Institute at Jogjakarta on Java.'

He opened another can of beer and went on, 'Have you heard of the Young Artists' style that's practised in Penestanan?'

Gael shook her head. 'No, what is it exactly?'

'It's a highly individual style of painting that was pioneered by a group of teenage boys back in the sixties, and it's getting to be world-famous.' He turned to look at her. 'Would you like to see how it's done?'

'Yes, very much.'

'Okay. We'll go up there tomorrow, and we'll stop at Ubud on the way. That's another place that's famous for painters.'

'Oh, but I ...' Gael broke off and looked at him rather helplessly. 'If you tell me where it is I could go alone. There's no need for you to ...' Her voice faded away as she saw the ironic look in his eyes.

'Ashamed to be seen out with me, Gael?'

She flushed; Dirk certainly didn't pull his punches. 'Certainly not—and you know it!' Her nervous fingers plucked some blades of grass and began to shred them. 'It's just that—well, that it might cause complications.'

'With your husband, d'you mean?' Dirk asked bluntly.

She became very still, gazing unseeingly at the ground. 'Yes.'

'Does he know you come here?'

Wordlessly she shook her head.

'Would he stop you coming if he found out?'

'Yes.'

'Because of me?'

'No, not because of you. Because—he just wouldn't want me to have this means of—of escape,' she said slowly.

Dirk took a sharp breath and said forcefully, 'If he treats you that badly why don't you leave him?'

Gael got quickly to her feet and took two agitated steps before Dirk caught her wrist and stopped her.

'I can't leave him! You don't understand.'

'So tell me.'

'No!' She realised that she had shouted the word at him

and tried to calm herself. 'Dirk, I understand that you want to help me, but there's nothing you can do. I have to stay with him for the time being.'

'Even though you were begging him for your freedom the other night?' he said harshly.

'Then you *did* see us? And you heard?'

'Sure I heard.' His hands came up to hold her arms. 'I'd gone to the Club specifically to find out who you were, and I admit that when I saw you go out into the garden I followed you.' His grip tightened. 'Has he been unfaithful to you, is that it?'

Gael looked away. She supposed you could call it that in a way. 'There is another woman in his life,' she admitted with a dry, mirthless laugh.

Dirk swore, shortly but effectively. 'Gael, I . . .'

She pulled away from him. 'Don't, Dirk, please. I—I just can't talk about it.'

'All right.' He came up behind her. 'But don't you think it's about time you started pulling yourself together? You can't go on wallowing in self-pity for the rest of your life, you know. Or is it that you enjoy playing the martyr?' he added brutally.

Gael swung round to face him, eyes wide with shock. 'What do you mean? I don't wallow in self-pity.'

'No? Then what do you call refusing to join the Country Club, avoiding the other wives' company like the plague, hiding away here, being afraid to be seen out in public with me? Everything points to the fact that you're running away because you're too big a coward to face up to the fact that your husband slept with another woman.'

She stared at him, white-faced. 'How do you know all that?'

He shrugged. 'The Club is a hotbed of gossip. I simply nodded in your direction and asked who was the lovely newcomer and I was inundated. Sift out fact from rumour and it wasn't difficult to find the truth.'

For a long moment she stood and gazed at him, then turned away and began to walk round the garden. Was she really running away? She supposed she must be. But Dirk didn't know the whole truth by any means, didn't know the unbearable humiliation and betrayal that she had suffered at Leo's hands. But maybe he was right in some ways, maybe she was letting the hurt rule her life too much. Retracing her steps, she came to where he was still standing watching her.

'All right, I will go with you tomorrow.'

His face betrayed nothing. 'Good. Don't bother to bring a picnic, we'll eat out. Now, come on, woman, back to work.' He gave her a light slap on her behind. 'I've got a deadline to keep even if you haven't.' And then he roared with laughter at the surprised look on her face and the way she instinctively covered her behind with her hands and ran indoors.

'But how are we going to get there if we don't go by car or bicycle?' Gael demanded.

She and Dirk were standing by the side of the road near the turn-off to the lane that led down to the plantation house. It was still quite early, but already the sun was hot enough to make her perspire even though she was wearing only a cotton sundress and a straw hat.

'You'll see. Ah, here it is.'

A car had come into sight round the bend and Dirk stepped into the road to wave it down. As it came nearer

Gael saw it was more like a van with windows let into the sides and an open back. She remembered having seen them before on the island but had no idea what they were. It drew up beside them and Dirk helped her to climb in through the back. A young, barefooted man was standing rather precariously on the dropped tailgate and Dirk spoke to him and gave him some money, then joined her on the long seats built along the sides of the vehicle. There were several other people already inside, women with the baskets they normally carried on their heads perched on their laps, a boy with a squealing piglet in his arms, as well as three men who grinned at her amiably. The man standing at the back shouted something and the vehicle started away.

Gael looked at Dirk in delighted surprise. 'It's a bus!'

'Of course. They're called *bemos*. There are hundreds of them all over Bali.'

It was the first of many interesting sights and experiences that day. They got off at a village where they watched women carrying offerings to the local temple on their heads: a great pile, often almost as tall as the women themselves, of fish, rice, cakes, flowers, fruits, eggs—and one woman even had a cooked chicken sitting triumphantly on top of her pile.

'What is it all for?' Gael asked in amazement, holding her breath in case any of the women lost their balance.

'It's the anniversary of their temple's consecration, the temple's birthday,' Dirk explained. 'They have a festival that lasts for three days, a mixture of religious ceremony and carnival. They have dances and a procession with several men inside lion or dragon costumes—similar to the long Chinese dragons. And they carry ornate, gilded umbrellas on long poles, and of course it's a great excuse to wear all their best and most colourful clothes.'

There were several foodstalls, *warung* Dirk called them, set up outside the main temple gate and here they ate their lunch in their fingers, long curled sausages, spicy dried fish which Gael turned down at first but Dirk insisted she try and which were in fact delicious; the meal finished off with guavas and a pineapple—the varieties of fruit were unimaginable. They watched people gambling at the roadside on a sort of tablecloth with the six sides of a dice printed on it. You placed your money on one of the number of dots, a real dice was thrown and if your symbol came up you won. Simple—and the banker couldn't lose. They stood aside to let a Gamelan orchestra of about thirty musicians march by, their instruments including gongs, drums, metal xylophones and a host of others Gael didn't recognise, all giving a rather high-pitched sound. Everything was bright and colourful and alive.

They spent some time in Penestanan watching the young painters at work. Some of them sat on the floor to work and all recreated the same style so exactly that sometimes two youths worked on the same painting. It was an individual style that Gael had never seen before; there was something almost Chinese in the precision of the layout, but the colours were purely Balinese, bright, vivid and full of life. Afterwards Dirk took her to a museum not far from the village where there was a collection of paintings by more traditional Balinese artists and she spent an engrossed hour comparing the two styles. The older paintings were crammed with detail, every inch of canvas utilised to show scenes from religious ceremonies, with very few landscapes or portraits.

Dirk pointed to part of a large picture. 'Look, that's the traditional Barong dance-drama. This is Rangda, the queen of the witches. And this is the Garuda bird, he's the mighty eagle who's supposed to carry the god Vishnu.' He put an arm casually across her shoulders and leaned close to her to indicate another section of the painting. 'And there are those ceremonial umbrellas I was telling you about.'

Gael leaned forward to look closer as he explained, their heads quite near together as he talked. She was so intent on the picture that the voices of the other people in the gallery hardly penetrated until they were close by and loud in her ears, and then she realised that they too were speaking English. They were women's voices and one of them sounded all too familiar!

Without looking round, Gael said in a fierce whisper, 'Let's go, quickly.' And she hurried out of the gallery. Dirk followed her at a more leisurely pace.

She didn't stop until she got right outside the building and then waited impatiently until Dirk joined her.

'Did you see those women?' she asked abruptly. 'I'm sure one was Norah Taylor. Do you know her?'

'Sure, everyone knows Norah.'

'Did she see us?' Her voice was anxious.

Dirk shrugged maddeningly. 'Does it matter?'

Gael frowned at him. 'Yes, it does matter. She doesn't like me.'

'Does she have cause?' Dirk fell into step beside her as they began to walk down the road.

With a sigh, Gael admitted honestly, 'Yes, I suppose she does. She came into my life at a time when—when I couldn't cope with people and I'm afraid I offended her right from the start. And now nothing would give her more pleasure than to be able to tittle-tattle to Leo about me. Especially as she fancies him herself.'

'And does he fancy her?'

'Good heavens, no! He isn't interested in anyone after . . .' She broke off, biting her lip.

'I don't think she saw us,' Dirk said into the silence. 'But does it matter if she did, and told your husband? Maybe it wouldn't do any harm to let him know that you have interests and friendships of your own. Or is he the possessive sort who believes that adultery is the male prerogative?'

'If you mean would he be jealous of anything I did, then the answer's no. But his career is wholly important to him and he'd be furious if he thought that there'd be any scandal.' Her voice filled with bitterness. 'He would certainly care about that!'

Dirk's Australian upbringing came to the fore. 'He sounds a right bastard. Why the hell did you marry him?'

Gael gave a mirthless laugh. 'Why does anyone get married? Because I was in love with him, of course.'

Catching her arm, Dirk swung her round to face him, his eyes intent. 'And now? Are you still in love with him?'

Her eyes became very cold. 'I hate him!' she said fiercely, then turned and hurried on down the road leaving him to follow after her.

Nothing more was said on the subject during their journey home, in a *dokar* this time, a horse-driven taxi with an awning over their heads to protect them from the sun, and again the next day Gael kept the conversation between them on strictly impersonal subjects. Dirk looked at her musingly, but he didn't try to extract any further confidences out of her, leaving her to tell him in her own time. She supposed that eventually, possibly just before she left Bali, she would put the record straight and tell him the whole truth, but not yet. Let him go on thinking that Leo had had an affair, even that was better than the truth.

She couldn't settle to her work very well that day and in the end exasperatedly pushed the canvas aside and took out a fresh one. Of its own volition her hand picked up a brush and began to paint in black, the strokes sure and purposeful. His features began to take form; the shape of his head; high forehead and straight nose, the determined thrust of his chin, the thick dark hair, and last of all his eyes, dark and alert. It was a portrait of Leo, but the Leo she had known in England, not in Bali. The face he had worn to deceive her and which she had fallen in love with. Gael stood and gazed at it for a long time, then took the canvas down and turned it with its face to the wall.

Back at the bungalow, she wheeled her bicycle into the shed and closed the door. They had no social engagement tonight so there would be plenty of time to take a leisurely bath before dinner.

'Hallo, Gael.'

At the sound of Leo's voice behind her, Gael dropped her handbag in fright. He straightened up from where he had been leaning against the veranda in the shade of a frangipani tree and crossed the few yards towards her. Calmly he bent to pick up her bag and held it out to her. She managed to take it, but her hands were shaking so much that she could hardly hold it.

Smoothly he said, 'I think we'd better have a little talk, don't you?' And putting his hand firmly beneath her elbow he led her into the house.

Once in the sitting-room he let go of her arm and turned to face her. 'The servants have left a cold meal for us in the dining-room. I told them they could go early tonight.'

A cold fear gripped her and she could only stand and stare at him, unable to speak.

His eyes ran over her, taking in her slim figure in the shorts and sun-top, her hair in the long pigtail. Surprisingly, when the question finally came he didn't sound angry.

'Where did you get the bike, Gael?'

There was no point in lying. 'I—I bought it.'

'And where did you get the money?'

'I sold my camera. At least, Pak Amat sold it for me. But you mustn't blame him,' she added hurriedly. 'I asked him to do it.'

'I have no intention of blaming him.' He paused. 'And where do you go on your bicycle?' he asked deliberately, his eyes watching her closely.

Gael turned away to put her handbag on the table. Desperately she wondered how much he knew. It could be pure chance that he happened to have come home early and caught her. She decided to try and brazen it out. Going to an armchair, she sat down and said as casually as she could, 'Oh, just around the island. Could I have a drink, please?'

Moving to the cabinet, he poured her a long, vermouth-based drink and carried it across to her. 'Oh, whereabouts on the island?'

She shrugged and curled her lip petulantly. 'All over the place. I like to draw the native villages and markets; that sort of thing. Not,' she added with a deliberate touch of nastiness in her voice, 'that it's anything to do with you where I go. So long as I keep to the bargain and act the company wife when necessary then I consider that the rest of the time is my own to do with as I like.'

To her amazement he nodded and said, 'I quite agree.' But then his eyes met hers and she grew suddenly ice-cold. 'So long as you keep to the bargain. But I don't consider having an affair with another man to be part of the deal!'

His voice lashed out like a whip and Gael cringed back in her chair. Oh God, he knew! *Damn* Norah! But still she tried to bluff because she was too terrified to do anything else. 'I—I don't know what you mean.'

'Oh, yes, you do.' Leo leaned forward and put a hand on either arm of the chair, his face angry now. 'Look at you, you've got guilt written all over your face. You go to meet him every day, don't you? *Don't you?*' He suddenly knocked the glass flying out of her hand and it smashed against the wall, the liquid leaving a dripping, spreading stain.

Gael looked at it in shocked horror for a moment, then ducked under his arm and ran for the French doors. Leo caught her before she had covered two yards.

'You'll tell me the truth, do you hear me?'

'What do you care?' Something seemed to snap inside her and Gael pulled away from him to glare up at his furious face. 'What the hell does it matter to you whether I'm having an affair or not? You're not interested in me, so why get angry when you think someone else is? Why don't you leave me alone and go back to yearning for your lost love?' she finished fiercely, her voice heavy with sarcasm.

'Leave Julia out of this!'

'Oh, yes,' Gael jeered derisively. 'We mustn't let anything dirty touch the whited sepulchre you've built around her, must we? Not that your beloved Julia was a paragon of virtue. *She* certainly wasn't above having an ...' Her furious voice broke off in mid-sentence as she suddenly realised what she was saying. Her hand went to her mouth in fear, but Leo hardly seemed to have heard.

'Don't try to get away from the subject. I should have

known you'd fall into bed with the first man that came along. The only thing that surprises me is that you've managed to keep it secret for so long. Or is it that he only wants you for sex and won't take you out much?' he added cruelly.

'I'm not having an affair!'

'Don't lie to me.' He caught hold of her arms and shook her roughly. 'You were ripe for a man's bed even before I married you,' he snarled. 'You almost begged to be taken that weekend we went sailing together.'

'That isn't true!' Gael began to struggle furiously, beating her fists against his chest and arching her body in a vain attempt to get free.

'Damn you! Is this what you want?' Suddenly Leo dragged her close against him, his eyes blazed down at her for a brief moment, and then his lips were on hers, kissing her with a brutal compulsion that forced her mouth open, forced every other thought out of her head. Instinct made her go on fighting him, but her struggles only seemed to inflame him further and he pressed her body hard against his own, his mouth moving against hers with a burning, bruising passion. His kiss made something inside her take fire and for a moment she yielded, consumed by need. Immediately his lips became more importuning, demanding a response, but suddenly she was fighting him again, her mind a mess of emotions as she kicked and writhed in his arms. He caught her wrists and held them behind her back, then bent her against his braced body and went on kissing her until at last she quietened and stood numbly within his arms.

At last he let her go, his breathing ragged, and stared down into her eyes, dark shadowed by emotion.

It was some time before either of them spoke and then Gael said huskily, 'I'm not having an affair.'

'How do you expect me to believe that?' Leo's voice was thick, uneven.

'It's really very simple,' Gael said clearly. 'Because I vowed that after what you did to me I'd never let a man touch me ever again!' Then she turned and ran out of the room leaving him staring after her.

Gael lay awake in bed most of that night. Leo had gone out shortly after their quarrel and she didn't hear the car return until well after midnight. By then she had come to the only decision she could possibly make; tomorrow she must go to the plantation house and collect all her things, tell Dirk that she wouldn't be going there any more. It was too dangerous, the risk too great for her to go on using the place. It would mean the loss of her studio and that would be hard to bear, but anything was better than running the risk of Leo changing his mind and making her stay with him longer.

The next morning she stayed in her room as usual until Leo had left and then came out to have breakfast and to tell Pak Amat that she wouldn't need a picnic lunch. Feeling tired and sad, she got on her bicycle and pedalled towards the Dutch house for the last time. She could imagine what Dirk would say about her decision; he had no time for what he would consider to be cowardice and would tell her to either stand up to Leo or leave him. But she couldn't leave him, and she was afraid to stand up to him again after last night. Her hand went up to her mouth that still felt bruised and sore from his brutal embrace. Why had he done that? Why? She could think of no reason other than to humiliate and cheapen her further. It certainly wasn't because he had wanted to, she thought bitterly. He had made that plain enough on numerous occasions.

A *bemo* heading for the next village passed her in a cloud of dust and a pair of monkeys scampered back into the forest as she came near them, but apart from that the road was empty and she made good time to the house. Dirk wasn't there, so she let herself in and dejectedly began to gather her things together, but presently she heard his whistle in the hall and then his steps on the landing.

'Hi. Coming for a swim?' His eyes ran over the empty worktable, the box of painting materials she had already packed, and his eyebrows rose questioningly.

'Dirk, I have to talk to you,' she said unhappily.

'Okay, but let's have our swim first, shall we?' He paused, then added pointedly, 'Who knows, you might even make it to the rocks and back today.'

Gael hesitated but then nodded. It might be easier to tell him out in the open air, away from the emotive atmosphere of her workroom. 'All right. I'll change.'

'Meet you in five minutes.'

He went out and Gael slipped out of her shorts and shirt. She hadn't brought a bikini, but the one she had worn a couple of days earlier was still on the balcony where she had left it to dry in the sun. She went out to get it, confident that no one could see her even though she was only wearing the briefest of bras and pants. Her fair hair fell loose about her shoulders; she would have to tie it up before she went swimming. The bikini was tied to the balcony by the straps and she bent to undo them, but as she did so a movement below caught her eye. Leo was standing in the garden staring up at her! For a heart-stopping moment she could only stand paralysed, rigid with shock. Then she

dropped the bikini and plunged back into the room just as
Leo ran towards the veranda steps.

'Dirk!' She ran into the corridor screaming his name and
headed for the landing, thinking that he was downstairs.
But he was in a room on the other side of the gallery and
came rushing out at her call, wearing only a pair of briefs,
like her in the middle of changing. He reached her near the
top of the staircase and caught hold of her as she babbled
incoherently.

'What is it? Gael, what's the matter?'

But then he heard Leo crash the door open and pound
up the stairs three at a time.

Gael clung to Dirk, afraid to let go. 'Don't let him touch
me. Oh, Dirk, I'm scared!'

'Take your hands off my wife!' Leo said savagely.

Dirk's arms closed round her protectively. 'Don't worry,
no one's going to hurt you while I'm around.' But he was
watching Leo, taking in the murderous rage on his face,
and he gently put Gael to one side.

The men faced each other angrily, like two wild beasts
about to fight to the bitter end, while Gael could only look
on helplessly. Dirk seemed more like an animal, almost
naked as he was, but somehow the fact that Leo was dressed
in conservative business suit and tie made the anger that
showed in his face all the more terrible.

She didn't see which one of them made the first move,
but suddenly they were hitting each other about the body
with a ferocity that terrified her.

They were both big men, and although Dirk was
broader, Leo had the advantage of being taller, but they
were both so angry that they didn't care where or how hard
they hit. Dirk landed a sickening blow in Leo's stomach

that made him grunt with pain, and suddenly Gael knew that she couldn't stand it any longer.

Running forward, she called out, 'Stop it! Stop it, both of you!' and tried to catch hold of their arms. But Leo had already drawn his fist back to return Dirk's blow and there was no way he could stop it. It caught Gael a stunning smash to the side of her face, delivered with all the force of his arm. Her eyes dilated and she staggered back, only half conscious. Suddenly there was nothing beneath her feet and she plunged down the staircase, rolling and crashing against the carved wooden banisters as she fell.

Above her she heard a voice call her name on a note of horror and fear, but then her head cracked heavily against a stair and she was unconscious before she reached the bottom and lay in a huddled, broken heap in the hall.

CHAPTER SEVEN

'My head! Oh, my head hurts so!'

'It's all right, darling. Don't try to talk. You'll soon be at the hospital.'

The voice above her went on reassuring her and she gradually became aware that she was lying in the back of a car, wrapped in a blanket, with her head pillowed against someone's shoulder. Other parts started to hurt: her legs, her shoulders, until she moaned aloud with pain.

'Hold on, darling. We're nearly there. Can't you go any faster?' This last remark was addressed to someone else in the front of the car, but she couldn't see who it was, couldn't see anything. The car hit a bump in the road that sent jagged pains through a thousand broken nerve ends. Gael gave a cry of agony and sank back over the abyss of oblivion.

It was a long time before she came to again and then the pain was gone, but her limbs felt strangely lifeless and so heavy that she couldn't move them. The room seemed dark and she couldn't see very well, but she could hear the air-conditioning whirring away and smell a peculiar antiseptic sort of odour. But the most pressing sensation was that of thirst. Her mouth was so dry and her throat felt parched. She moved restlessly on the pillow, but at once her head began to throb and she gave a little whimper of pain. It seemed an age of mounting loneliness and fear before any-one came, and then it was a nurse, a native woman in a starched white uniform who opened the door to let in a shaft of light and crossed over to her bedside.

She saw that Gael was awake and smiled. 'Hallo, Mrs Kane. I expect you'd like a drink.' She lifted her up and helped her to drink thirstily from a glass of water. 'I'll go and fetch Dr Stanton.'

Gael lay back on the pillows and tried to think. She was evidently in the local European hospital, but why she was there and what was wrong with her she couldn't for the life of her remember, and her head hurt so much when she tried to concentrate that the pain blinded her.

The door opened again and the nurse came back accom-panied by Tom Stanton. He sat on the edge of the bed, picked up her wrist to feel her pulse, and smiled at her.

'Can you see me all right, Gael?'

'Yes. But—but it's dark in here.'

'Open the blinds a little more, nurse, and see if that's any better.'

Shafts of sunlight broke through the dimness and Gael saw that she was in a largish room, luxuriously appointed for a hospital, with a television set in a corner, several comfortable chairs and a view through the window to the beautifully maintained gardens.

'My head hurts,' she said fretfully.

'I'm not surprised. That's quite a bump you've got. But you're a lucky girl, there's no bones broken, although you're going to hurt all over for quite a while yet and you'll have an interesting pattern of bruises before very long.' He looked at her more keenly. 'Can you remember what happened?'

'No.' She went to shake her head, but then realised that there was a bandage round it. Tentatively she tried to reach up to touch it, but her arm felt like lead.

'Better not try to move. I've given you a shot to deaden the pain and let you get some sleep. You've just got a cut on your forehead. Nothing serious, and it won't leave a scar,' he added reassuringly. He stood up. 'Leo's outside waiting to see you. Been there for quite some time, but I'm only going to let him in for five minutes and then you must go to sleep.'

Leo! Suddenly memory came crashing back and she saw again the fury in his face when he had seen her with Dirk.

'No!' She looked up at Tom Stanton, her eyes wide and scared. 'No, I—I don't want to see him. *Please!*'

'Nurse, wait for me outside.' He waited until the nurse had gone then looked at Gael with a frown. 'Gael, what is it? Do you remember now what happened to you? Is it something to do with Leo?'

Gael gazed up at him wretchedly, uncertain what to say, how much to tell him. 'It's just that I—don't feel up to seeing anyone now,' she mumbled at length, turning her head away.

The doctor continued to frown down at her for a moment and then nodded. 'All right, don't worry about it. I'll talk to him, tell him you're not well enough yet.'

He left her alone, a slim, still figure in the impersonal hospital bed, and it seemed like light years before the sedative took effect and sleep pushed the anguished pictures out of her mind.

It was light again when she woke early the next morning and the nurse who came when she pressed the bell over her bed told her that she'd slept the clock round. But the sleep had done nothing to lessen her anxieties and the pain-killer they had given her had worn off. Her body seemed like one big ache all over so that she couldn't get comfortable no matter which position she tried to lie in.

Dr Stanton came to see her after breakfast and asked her how she felt.

Gael gave him rather a sour smile. 'I feel as if I've gone fifteen rounds with a heavyweight boxer and lost the fight,' she answered, trying to keep her voice light.

He began to check her pulse again. 'And have you—been in a fight?'

Gael jumped and her eyes quickly slid from his. 'N-no, of course not. I—I fell down the stairs.'

'Really?' His voice was dry. 'I thought you lived in a bungalow?'

Her hand began to shake no matter how hard she tried to control it. 'I wasn't at home at the time.'

He let go her hand. 'Leo's been on the phone. He wants

to know when he can come and see you.'

Head lowered, her hands nervously pleating the edge of the sheet, she said unsteadily, 'It really does hurt and I—I can't get comfortable. Couldn't you give me another sedative? I'm still very tired.'

Tom Stanton looked at her for a long moment, noting the high flush on her cheeks, her shaking hands, and the way she wouldn't look him in the eyes. 'All right,' he said abruptly. 'Maybe sleep is the best thing for you at the moment. I'll send the nurse in with some tablets presently.'

Gael still didn't look at him, but there was gratitude in her voice as she thanked him.

He moved to the door and then looked back. 'Oh, by the way, you should never tell lies when someone's taking your pulse—they can always feel it.'

Later that day they brought her in some flowers that Leo had sent, a basket full of dark red roses that must have cost the earth. A typically ostentatious present for an executive officer to send his sick wife, Gael thought cynically as soon as she saw them, and told the nurse to take them away.

'But they are beautiful,' the girl exclaimed.

'I don't like them,' Gael retorted. 'They look like blood.' And she turned to stare unseeingly out of the window.

There were other flowers and a basket of fruit from colleagues of Leo's, sent because they thought it was their duty, she supposed, and she let these stay, but when Leo sent her another bouquet the next morning, of mixed flowers this time, she again had them taken away. Afterwards Tom Stanton came in to see her, his face grim.

'Gael, Leo's in my office. He wants to see you.' She opened her mouth to speak, but he went on, 'And it's no good you making another excuse. We both know that you're well enough to start having visitors, and he has the right to see you.' He looked at her averted face. 'Can I tell him to come in?'

'No, please.' She looked up at him helplessly. 'I don't want to see him, Tom.'

'Why not? What's he done to you?' When she didn't answer he said forcefully. 'Gael, you've got to tell me the truth. You've been frightened and nervous ever since you came to Bali. I noticed it the first time I met you, and I also saw the bruises on your arms. I thought then that Leo might have hurt you.' Almost reluctantly he asked, 'Is that what it is, Gael? Does Leo beat you?'

Eyes wide in her suddenly pallid face, Gael stared up at him. Here it was, given to her on a plate, the perfect excuse to get away from Leo, to never have to see him again. If she said yes, Tom Stanton would keep Leo away from her, help her to get a passport so that she could leave Bali. She would be free, that wonderful, wonderful word. Then her mind ran on, imagining the scandal it would cause, no matter how discreetly it was handled. Leo might well be allowed to keep his job, but he would never live down the scandal, the gossip would follow him everywhere he went. Well, it served him right, didn't it, after the way he had mistreated her? She thought of all he stood to lose on top of what he had already lost, and knew suddenly that she couldn't do it. Even in her fury she hadn't been able to hurt him by telling him of his fiancée's betrayal with another man, and she couldn't betray him now by taking the easy way out.

Stolidly she said, 'I fell down the stairs.'

'I see.' Dr Stanton straightened up. 'Then you have no reason for refusing to see Leo.'

Tears welled into her eyes and she looked at him pleadingly. 'Please, Tom, not today. I'll ... perhaps tomorrow.'

He ran a hand through his thinning hair and sighed. 'All right, have it your way. But I'm not going to be able to hold him off much longer, Gael.'

He went away and the nurse brought her lunch and then came back an hour later to collect the tray and found it untouched. Gael sat in a chair by the window, her legs curled up under her, her mind miles away. They had removed the bandage round her head now and replaced it with a small dressing that was almost hidden by her hair. The pains had mostly gone but she still felt stiff and sore, especially on her hips and shoulders which seemed to have taken the worst of her fall. She knew that she was really well enough to leave the hospital, that she couldn't put off seeing Leo much longer. But her whole being shrank away from the thought, not because she was afraid he would do her any physical violence. No, it wasn't that. So why? Why was she so afraid to see him again?

Her reverie was suddenly broken as she heard the window start to open and then it was pushed wide as Dirk put a leg over the sill and sprang easily into her room.

He gave her his usual grin. 'A fly will go in your mouth if you leave it open like that.' Hastily Gael closed it and he said approvingly, 'That's better,' and bent to kiss her.

Afterwards he drew back and looked at her bemused face. 'Hm, that's quite a bruise you've got. How does the rest of you shape up in comparison?'

'I have every shade from light blue through to black,' Gael told him dryly.

'Serves you right,' Dirk told her unsympathetically. 'Hasn't anyone taught you never to walk in on a fight? You broke it up just as it was getting interesting, too.'

Tartly she said, 'Anyone would think that you were enjoying it?'

'As a matter of fact I was. Haven't had a good fight in years. And that husband of yours is just about my weight.' Then he laughed at her outraged face and said, 'Here, I've brought you a present,' and handed her a can of beer, opening another for himself.

Gael looked at him helplessly, not knowing whether to laugh or cry. A surge of warmth filled her; he was the only friend she had and she knew that she would always remember him with gratitude and affection.

Something of her feelings must have shown on her face, because Dirk sat down opposite her and became unusually serious. 'They told me that you weren't allowed any visitors, but I had to come and talk to you. Gael, I have to know—are you sure you're no longer in love with Leo Kane,' he paused, 'or he with you? The way he came after you ...'

Gael shook her head tiredly. 'He never loved me, Dirk. He only married me because his fiancée had been killed and he needed a wife in order to get this job. We were married on the day we left England to come here and he told me the truth when we arrived.'

Dirk stared at her in stupefaction. 'Are you telling me what I think you are? That he's never even ...'

'That he's never made love to me, do you mean? No, he hasn't,' she admitted baldly. 'Not that *love* would have entered into it.'

Dirk frowned. 'But why did you let me believe that he'd had an affair with another woman?'

She shrugged. 'Because it was easier than admitting the truth. And because it was true in a way; he is in love with another woman, only she happens to be dead!' she added wretchedly.

Dirk was silent for a moment but then said firmly, 'What you've told me only makes what I came to say easier.' He looked at her intently. 'Gael, I want you to leave him and come to me. Don't say anything yet—just hear me out. I know there's a hell of a difference in our ages, but we seem pretty compatible and I'm sure we could work it out. Okay, I know I'm no great catch, but I could provide for you, give you a home.' Rather sheepishly he added, 'As a matter of fact the plantation house belongs to me, I just had the villa built because the old house was too big and inconvenient for one man alone. But we could open it up again if you want—I make more than enough money from my writing to do that.' Clumsily he reached forward and took her hands. 'I know you're not in love with me, but I promise you that you'd be happier with me than you are now, although I'm not going to promise not to make any demands on you—I couldn't live in the same house with you and not want you.' He broke off. 'Well, I guess that's it. Will you leave him and come to me?'

There were tears running unheeded down Gael's cheeks as she reached out to gently touch his face. 'Dear Dirk! You don't know how good you are for my morale. You're a very wonderful friend.'

'Friend?'

'Yes.' She blinked hard and said unsteadily, 'I can't leave Leo yet, but even if I could I'd want to be by myself, to stand on my own two feet. I'm afraid I'm rather off men at the moment,' she added with a travesty of a smile. 'But I shall always remember that you offered to come to my rescue and I'm really very grateful for your kindness, Dirk. Truly.'

His grip tightened on her hand as he said roughly, 'Kindness doesn't come into it. Do you think I make a habit of offering my house to girls whose marriages are in trouble? I love you, Gael. I fell in love with you the moment I saw you lying asleep in my garden.'

'Oh, Dirk! I didn't know.' She shook her head helplessly, angrily almost, because she knew she had to hurt him. 'I'm sorry. I'm very fond of you and you're very dear to me, but I couldn't live with you when I don't love you. I know what it's like to live with someone who doesn't love you, and it wouldn't work, Dirk, I just know it wouldn't.'

'We could *make* it work,' he said forcefully. 'If we both wanted it enough.'

'No, I'm sorry, more sorry than I can say.' She made a helpless gesture with her free hand. 'But when I leave Leo it will be to lead my own life. I never want to be dependent on a man for my happiness again.'

He straightened up and let go her hand. 'All right, but I'm not going to leave it there,' he said grimly. 'You're too emotionally mixed up to think straight at the moment, but I'm going to make sure that I'm around when you finally work things out. And just promise me one thing, will you?' he added, looking at her earnestly. 'That if you ever need it you'll come to me for help. And there's no strings attached to it. You don't have to feel that you'll have to stay with me if I help you.' For a second his usual grin showed through. 'Not that I won't have a damn good try at persuading you, but I'll be there any time you need me.'

'Thanks, Dirk.' She reached out to touch his hand. 'You don't know how much that means to me.'

His big hand covered her small one. Urgently he said, 'Leave him, Gael. Can't you see he's destroying you?'

'I will—soon. But not yet, I can't leave yet.'

'Little fool!' He didn't try to persuade her any more, just bent to kiss her again and left the same way as he had come.

Gael watched him go, her brain in a turmoil. Was she being a fool not to accept his offer? Her mouth set into a thin, bitter line. It seemed that everyone was offering her ways to get away from Leo today. There ought to be a banner with 'HOW TO LEAVE LEO DAY' written on it hung across the room, she thought cynically. But she had turned both openings down. Why, because she'd given her word to stay for six months? Because breaking her promise would bring her down to his level? She got up and began to pace restlessly up and down the room, the soreness in her legs unheeded. My God, she thought, am I some sort of masochist that I can even contemplate going back to live with Leo when I can't find the courage to even see him? She caught hold of the back of a chair and gripped it until her knuckles showed white. It was no use. Nothing was any use any more. She couldn't hurt Leo more than he'd been hurt already, no matter how much he deserved that she should walk out on him. The two offers of help she had had only served to convince her of that, so there was no alternative but to go back and to live out the days until he saw fit to give her her freedom. Long days without the solace of Dirk's company or her work. But somehow she had to get through them, somehow.

Day turned into night and the nurse took away another untouched meal. There were the usual hospital sounds in the corridor outside, voices, trolleys being pushed along, footsteps of visitors coming and going, but Gael took little notice of them. She was standing by the window, with a long candlewick dressing-gown in her favourite peach colour over her nightdress. She had been standing there for some time, leaning against the wall and gazing out at the sunset, but the sun's rays had been gone for a long time now and there was nothing to see beyond the light cast by her window. Even raised voices and a commotion in the corridor didn't disturb her, until her door was flung violently open and Leo burst in with a nurse and an orderly at his heels.

Gael swung round to stare at him, her hands going to her throat in sudden fear. Leo took a hasty step forward and then stopped when he saw her white face. His face, too, was strained and he looked tired, as if he hadn't been sleeping well.

'I have to talk to you,' he said shortly. 'Tell them to go away—please.'

For a long moment Gael didn't move, then she slowly nodded to the anxious-looking attendants. 'It—it's all right.'

When they had gone she turned her back on him, but found that she could see his reflection in the dark panes of the window. He was looking at her with a strange expression on his face, one she had never seen before and couldn't fathom. He thrust his hands in his pockets as if he couldn't trust himself not to touch her, and came nearer.

'I'm sorry to burst in on you when you're not well, but I wasn't going to let them keep me out any longer. I had to see you—to apologise first of all for what happened.' His voice became urgent. 'I didn't mean to hurt you, Gael. You must believe that.'

She looked down at her hands. 'No, I know. It's all right, it doesn't matter.'

For once he seemed lost for words, uncertain. 'While you've been in here I've done a lot of thinking—about us, about the situation between us. I've treated you badly, I know, and I was crazy to think that by bringing you here I'd make you atone for what you'd done. Crazy to even want to.' He shrugged helplessly. 'But there it is. Men sometimes do mad things when they're in the grip of strong emotions. They want to lash out at someone because they're powerless to do anything else. And I'm afraid you got in the way—figuratively and literally.'

He came up close behind her and he saw that she was watching his reflection in the glass. Their eyes met, and held, and suddenly Gael knew why she had been so afraid to see him; it was because she couldn't bear to see the hate and anger in his eyes when he looked at her, the fury in his face when he had caught her with Dirk. But there was nothing of those emotions in his eyes now, just a strange, almost haunted look, coupled with an uncertainty that was wholly alien to him.

Abruptly she turned away and walked further into the room. 'What are you trying to say?'

Leo straightened and said more confidently, 'That I want us to try and start all over again, right from the beginning. As people who've just met and are getting to know each other. To try and forget what happened between us if that's possible and . . .'

'It isn't possible!' Gael broke in vehemently. 'How could anyone ever forget what you did to me—what you believe I did to you?'

His jaw tightened and he stepped quickly up to her. 'We could try. All right, it would be hard, perhaps damn near impossible, but I desperately want us to try, Gael.' Earnestly he went on, 'Surely you can see that we can't go on living together in the atmosphere we've . . .'

'We don't have to go on living together at all,' Gael broke in caustically.

A shutter came down over his face. 'What do you mean?' he demanded shortly.

'I mean that you can let me go. Give me my freedom.'

'So that you can go and live with Dirk Vanderman?' he said with scarcely controlled violence.

A flicker of surprise showed in her eyes and although she hid it quickly, it was too late.

'He's asked you, hasn't he?' Leo demanded fiercely.

Anger overcame discretion. 'So what if he has?'

Face taut, he said slowly, 'Are you in love with him? Are you?' He reached out suddenly and caught her by the shoulders, turning her round to face him when she tried to move away. 'Gael, I have to know.'

'Take your hands off me! Don't touch me!' Her voice rose sharply and he immediately let go, his face white.

'I'm sorry, I didn't mean to—to handle you.'

Gael looked at him uncertainly, recognising the restraint he was putting on himself but not knowing what to make of his changed attitude. She opened her mouth to speak, but before she could do so the door burst open again and Tom Stanton hurried in.

'Gael, are you all right? The nurses heard shouting. If he's ...'

But Leo showed no restraint towards the doctor. 'Get out of here, Stanton, I'm talking to my wife,' he commanded curtly.

Tom gazed at him in open-mouthed astonishment. No one had ever spoken to him like that in his own hospital before. Then he surrendered to the inevitable. Looking at

Gael, he said stiffly, 'I'll be outside in the corridor if you need me.'

When he had gone there was a long silence until Gael again turned her back on Leo and said dully, 'I'm not in love with Dirk. And I don't want to go and live with him.'

'But he asked you to?'

'Yes.'

'When?'

'This—this afternoon. He came to see me.'

'I see.'

She turned to look at him and saw that his lips had thinned. 'I didn't ask to see him, if that's what you're thinking. He came through the window.'

To her surprise Leo looked amused. 'Now why didn't I think of that?' But then his face hardened as he said, 'But he's in love with you.' It was a statement, not a question.

Gael looked away. 'That's none of your business.'

There was anger in his voice suddenly, raw and sharp. 'And I suppose the fact that he's your lover isn't my business either?' He swung her round to face him, holding her against the wall, his hands imprisoning hers. 'Look at me, Gael! Is he your lover or isn't he?'

Gazing up into his face, Gael suddenly remembered the way he had kissed her the day before he had found her with Dirk. She shivered suddenly and had to fight back tears. Angrily she said, 'It doesn't matter whether I deny it or not, does it? You'll still go on believing what you want to believe, and quite frankly I don't much care one way or the other. Now will you please let go of me? You're hurting my wrists.'

Leo did as she asked but didn't move away. His eyes had an unexpectedly dejected look in them as he said slowly,

'We just don't seem to be able to have a rational talk without tearing each other to pieces.' He looked down at his hands. 'And no matter how much I promise myself that I won't touch you I still ...' He broke off and deliberately took a few paces away from her. 'Will you come back to the bungalow?'

'Will you give me my freedom?' Gael countered.

His lips thinned. 'No, not yet.'

She said flatly, 'Then I don't have any choice, do I?'

He looked at her with a frown. 'Gael, I ...'

'Oh, why don't you go away? You've got what you came for, haven't you? The avoidance of a scandal that might endanger your career?'

'That wasn't my reason for coming,' he interrupted urgently. 'I wanted to ...'

'Will you please go!' Biting her lip, Gael tried to keep her voice even. 'Please, Leo, I'm very tired.'

He looked at her grimly for a moment and then nodded. 'All right. I'll come and collect you tomorrow morning.'

Dully she turned away. 'Yes, all right.'

Leo stood and looked at her drooping figure and seemed as if he was about to say something more, but then opened the door and closed it behind him with a decisive click.

He called for her promptly at nine the next morning, bringing her handbag and some clothes: a blue linen, sleeveless shirtwaister dress, matching sandals, and underclothes, of course: a white waist slip, bra and pants. Gael felt a sudden surge of embarrassment knowing that he had touched such intimate garments, must have gone through her things to find them. Slowly she dressed and put on her make-up, feeling very reluctant to leave what had become the sanctuary of the hospital and face the outside world.

She realised how easy it must be to become institutional-
ised, to live a life without any responsibilities, where you
never had to make any decisions. As she brushed her hair
she studied her reflection in the mirror. How different she
looked from a few months ago! Even if one discounted the
plaster on her forehead and the bruising on the side of her
face, she still looked older, sadder, a dark, fed-up look in
the blue eyes that had once sparkled with youth and the joy
of living.

Leo was waiting in the reception area and immediately
came to take her suitcase from the nurse who was escort-
ing her. His eyes flickered over her, but then he turned to
thank the nurse before taking Gael's arm and leading her
out to the car. Silently he helped her in and then tossed the
case in the back. To her surprise he didn't turn into the
road leading to the bungalow but headed in the opposite
direction, away from the coast.

In answer to her startled look, he said easily, 'I thought
we might take a drive up into the mountains.'

'What about your work?'

He gave a somewhat wry grin. 'I think they'll be able to
manage without me for one day.'

They didn't talk much as they drove along, Leo concen-
trating on weaving the car through the usual Balinese
traffic: *bemos*, cyclists, ramshackle trucks, *dokars* and the
occasional tourist bus, but presently, as the villages were
left behind in the plain and the road climbed higher, there
was less traffic to negotiate and he fumbled in his pocket
for a cigarette.

'Light me one, will you?'

He tossed her the packet and Gael lit one from the car
lighter and passed it to him.

'Thanks.' It was inevitable that their fingers touched as

she handed it to him, but she instantly drew away. Leo's lips twisted wryly, but his voice was quite casual as he said, 'We've received rather an interesting invitation.'

'Oh. To the Country Club?'

'No, something quite different. It's from Kartini and Pak Amat. It seems that their son will be fifteen soon and in a few days there'll be a celebration to mark his change from boyhood to manhood. If what I gather from them is correct, the way they do it is to have the boy's upper teeth filed to form a straight line. They believe that by doing this several of his bad qualities will be diminished and the boy will grow up to be a better man.'

'File his teeth!' Gael exclaimed. 'But isn't it terribly painful?'

'Well, I must say it sounds a bit drastic and at first I thought of refusing because I didn't think you'd want to watch it, but it seems that it's quite a high honour for a foreigner to be asked, so I'm afraid we don't have much choice if we don't want to offend Kartini and Pak Amat.'

'I wondered why all the Balinese men had such even smiles,' Gael remarked wonderingly. 'It's rather an extreme method, isn't it?'

Leo shrugged. 'All races have some sort of ceremony or other; the Jews with their Bar Mitzvahs, us with our coming-of-age parties and the thing about getting the key of the door, although that's almost died out now.' He glanced at her and smiled. 'Don't worry, you can always close your eyes if you don't want to look.' Over-casually he added, 'You could even hold my hand if it would help.'

Her eyes flew to his and for a moment their glances held, but then she quickly looked away. 'Are we nearly there?' she asked sharply.

'Almost. Look, you can see Mount Batur on our right

now. There should be a side-road leading up to Kintamani somewhere along here.'

The air was fresh and cool after the humid atmosphere of the plain. Gael took great breaths of it as they walked from the tourists' car park across to the restaurant complex built on the slopes of the volcano.

'Feels good, doesn't it?' Leo remarked. 'Let's take a walk along there and have a look at the view before lunch, shall we?'

Paths with panoramic view points had been cut into the mountainside and there were several tourists, Australians mostly from their accents, walking towards them, cameras at the ready. They strolled unhurriedly along until Gael gave an involuntary exclamation of delight as they rounded a bend and saw a large lake set in a fold of the mountains, its surface like a carpet of blue sapphires that shimmered in the sunlight.

'Oh, how lovely! How I'd love to paint that!'

'Well, I can't provide a palette and easel, but I can provide this.' Leo took a rather bulky object from his pocket and handed it to her.

It was a camera, a small, compact but highly expensive model.

'It's got a film in it,' he told her. 'And the light meter is automatic so you just point the thing and press the button.'

Gael looked at him uncertainly for a moment, then gave a little shrug before lifting the camera to her eyes. She took several shots of the view and of the volcano.

'When did the mountain erupt last?' she asked idly as she photographed the peak.

Just as casually, Leo answered, 'In 1974,' and then laughed at the expression of horror on her face. 'Don't worry, if it was going to blow again we'd get plenty of warning.'

He continued to smile at her as Gael gazed at him, but in a different kind of shock; he was so different, treating her almost as if—as if he liked her, wanted to be with her. He had never laughed or joked with her since he had dropped the act he had put on to get her here. Abruptly she held the camera out to him.

'Thank you for lending it to me,' she said curtly.

But Leo made no attempt to take it. 'It's yours. I bought it to replace the one you sold.' He paused, but when she didn't speak, only looked at him in amazement, he went on, 'And I've opened an account for you at my bank. An allowance will be paid into it every month and you can draw on it straight away, and if there's anything special you want you only have to ask.'

Gael stared at him blankly, unable to take in his complete volte-face. 'Why?' she exclaimed. 'Why are you doing this?'

Leo took a purposeful stride towards her and said earnestly, 'I told you last night that I realised how badly I've treated you. I'm just trying to put things right, to make amends, if you like.'

'With money?' Gael interrupted harshly.

'That's only a part of it. I never intended you to be without it, you could always have come to me if you needed anything and I . . .'

Gael laughed mirthlessly. 'Oh, that's really funny! You lie and cheat and threaten me with physical violence and then expect me to come to you when I need something?' She glared at him balefully. 'I'd rather die than ask you for anything! Especially money! I may have to live under your roof and eat the food you provide, but if you think I'd touch a penny of your rotten money . . .' She broke off, her breathing uneven, her face pale so that the bruises on the side of her face showed up vividly against her pallid skin. 'And anyway, what makes you think that if I've got money I won't use it to try and get away from you?'

Leo lifted up his hands as if he wanted to get hold of her arms but when he realised what he was doing a muscle in his jaw tightened and he thrust them into his pockets.

Almost curtly he replied, 'Because you promised you would stay with me for six months.'

Unsteadily she said, 'And you think I'd keep that promise—even if I had a chance to leave you?'

Slowly he said, 'You already had that chance—and you didn't take it.'

Gael bit her lip and looked away. 'No.'

His eyes intent, Leo said, 'Why didn't you go to Vanderman, Gael? Even if you weren't in love with him it would have got you away from me.'

'You mean why didn't I use him the same way you used me?' Blue eyes flashed with anger. 'Just because you've sunk low enough to do it you think that everyone else ought to be on your level. Well, I'm not! Even though I'm desperate to get away from you, even though the last two months have been pure hell!'

They were both silent for a long moment; Gael angry and defiant, Leo with a grim, set look on his face. Then his eyes settled on the dark bruises on her cheek and he slowly reached up and touched them, so gently that she hardly felt it, but even so she flinched.

His voice sounding strange, he said slowly, 'Gael, that day I found you with him . . .'

'I don't want to talk about it,' she broke in fiercely.

'*But I must.* When I saw you fall down the stairs, when I knew that you were hurt, thought that you might even be ...' His face paled and he had to take a grip of himself before he could go on. 'Well, something seemed to suddenly snap inside me and all the hate, all the bitterness I'd felt over Julia's death—every last vestige of it seemed to just melt away.' He shook his head helplessly. 'It was as if I'd wakened up after a long and terrible nightmare, one in which the world had been turned upside down and I'd lost all sense of proportion and justice. When I saw you fall I realised a whole lot of things that I'd been completely blind to before.'

He would have gone on, but Gael broke in sarcastically, 'So you woke up out of your nightmare? Well, bully for you! I wish I could say the same, but unfortunately I'm still having to live through mine!'

Leo gave a harsh, exasperated sigh and there was a bleak look in his eyes as he said, 'The money's there; use it or not, as you wish. Now, let's go and have lunch, shall we? And perhaps if we stick to impersonal subjects we'll manage not to tear each other to pieces for the duration of the meal,' he added grimly.

They managed it—just, although the tension between them came very close to erupting again several times, and it was really only saved by sheer will-power on Leo's part, a determination not to be drawn into a fight. And that determination was carried on after they returned to the bungalow; he insisted on talking to her as if they were on friendly terms, telling her about the hospital project, suggesting places they might visit together on the island, and refusing to rise whenever she made a jibe at him. His attitude confused her and she didn't know how to deal with it. Before, everything had been clear cut—they hated each other and that was that, but now Leo seemed to have changed almost over night, although, when she came to think about it, he had been less obviously antagonistic towards her for some time, but she had been so busily feeding her hatred for him that she had hardly noticed.

She distrusted the new situation, was afraid of it almost, and so tried to make him reveal his hatred of her again by goading him into losing his temper. That there was a certain element of fascination in seeing how far she could go she wouldn't admit even to herself. Once she thought she had succeeded in pushing him over the edge as he rounded on her after some jeering retort that had cut deep, his eyes savage in his taut face, but after a moment when she had cringed with sudden fear, he had turned on his heel and strode sharply out of the room, slamming the door behind him.

Gael had known then that her ploy wasn't going to work, that Leo had beaten her in this as he had beaten her in everything else, and that she was going to have to try to come to terms with the new situation. She became quiet and withdrawn, no longer trying to rile him, and watching him with puzzled eyes when she thought he wasn't looking, turning hastily away when he glanced up suddenly and caught her. Unfortunately it was the weekend the day after she left the hospital and Leo insisted on taking her for a drive round a new part of the island, stopping for a swim at an almost deserted cove during the hottest part of the day. And on Sunday he took her to Sanur beach where they hired a native outrigger, a *prao*, and sailed to Turtle Island, a small island named after the many giant turtles that lived out their long, long lives on its peaceful shores beneath the tropical sun.

It was all very confusing, and for the life of her Gael couldn't think why his attitude had changed, but she was certain that there had to be an ulterior motive; he had deceived her so much before that no way could she believe the reasons he had given.

On Monday morning she came out of the bathroom after taking a shower just as Leo emerged from his room. Instinctively Gael pulled her bathrobe closer about her, conscious of her nakedness beneath it. She went to hurry past him, but he reached across in front of her and put his hand on the wall, barring her way.

'Good morning,' he said pleasantly. 'Did you sleep well?' then waited so that she had to answer him.

'Yes, I suppose so,' she admitted ungraciously.

'Good, then come and have breakfast with me.'

Before she could object he swept her out to the patio and a grinning Pak Amat went running to fetch a place setting for her.

'Will you do the honours?' Leo asked, indicating the coffee pot.

Reluctantly Gael poured the coffee, watching Leo suspiciously as he gravely passed her the cream and sugar, but his face was completely impassive.

'How would you like to come up to the hospital site with me today?' he asked offhandedly as he began to eat the scrambled eggs Pak Amat brought him.

Gael's eyes opened wide in surprise. 'But—but surely there isn't anything to see yet?'

'Not on the ground, no. But I thought you might be interested to see the model of how the complex should look

when it's finished. And I could use your advice on the art-
work we intend to commission for a wall in the main
entrance and also for the small temple that will be incor-
porated into the complex.'

'Why me?' she asked, her puzzlement increasing.

Lightly he answered, 'You're the art expert.'

'Not on Balinese art, and that's what you want, isn't it?'

'Yes, but I'm quite sure you could soon learn.' He leaned
forward. 'It's within my province to appoint someone who
will decide on what artwork we need, commission the pieces
and make sure they're finished on time. The job is yours, if
you want it.' Persuasively he added, 'I'll put a car at your
disposal and you can travel all over the island, search out
all the artists' colonies, choose what you want—as long as
it stays within the budget, of course. But, subject only to
that restriction, you'll have carte blanche.'

Gael's eyes lit up eagerly. It was a dream of a job, one in
which she knew she would find extreme pleasure and fulfil-
ment. But it was Leo who was offering it to her. Why, as a
bribe to stay?

Flatly she said, 'I wouldn't be here long enough to see the
project through.'

He shrugged slightly. 'But you'd have four months in
which to sort out what you want and put the work in hand.
Then I'd have to find someone else to take over.'

Gael looked at him, suspicious of his offer, suspicious of
this whole cosy domestic scene of breakfasting together in
the early morning sun, conversing over the coffee cups.
Abruptly she set hers down and stood up.

'I'll think about it,' she said shortly.

'But you'll come up to the site today?'

'No,' shaking her head, 'not today.'

She went to walk back into the house, but as she passed him Leo caught her wrist.

'Gael, you don't have to be afraid to accept. To work for the company isn't taking anything from me. You'll be standing on your own feet, making your own mistakes. And if I don't like the way you're handling things, then I'll tell you, just as I'd tell any other employee. But you'd have an interest, you wouldn't be tied to the house.' When she didn't answer he gave her wrist a little shake. 'Can't you see what I'm trying to do? Won't you at least try to meet me halfway?'

Gael looked down into the dark eyes that regarded her so urgently. 'Yes, I can see what you're trying to do. I just don't know *why*,' she added balefully. 'And I'm not sure that I'd take even one step towards you even if I did!'

She had gone inside to dress then and Leo drove off without her, leaving her with her emotions in a crazy mixture of distrust and longing. How she would love that job! In any other circumstances she would have been on fire with excitement just at the thought of it.

As it was their son's coming of age celebration the next day, Gael let Pak Amat and Kartini go home soon after breakfast and spent the rest of the day in brooding thought, her only interruptions several phone calls from some other company wives who had heard she was out of hospital and called to enquire how she was feeling. Gael could sense the curiosity behind their questions, although no one was blatant enough to come right out and ask her what had happened until Norah Taylor phoned early in the afternoon.

'I do hope no lasting damage,' Norah asked purringly. 'We heard you were badly cut and bruised around the face?'

Gael demurred, but the woman went on, 'One has to be so careful in this climate. Tempers can so easily become overheated, and although Leo might tolerate your—er—behaviour in England, in Bali he obviously isn't able to control himself quite so well.'

Gael gave an outraged gasp, but Norah continued to snipe at her, each comment or question intended to cut and fester, until Gael gave up trying to protest and just slammed the phone down on her. The cat! The nasty, scandalmongering old cat! Seething indignation filled her for the rest of the day and it was in a belligerent mood that she prepared dinner and snapped out at Leo that she wasn't promising anything but she would go to the site with him the next morning. Then she shut herself away in her room as usual and spent one of the worst nights she had known since she came to Bali—and heaven knew there had been bad nights enough!

The trip to the site she found both fascinating and frustrating. Fascinating because the job was on a larger scale and even more exciting than she had imagined, and frustrating because she couldn't completely give herself to the project as she longed to, nor even overtly show her feelings about it. While Leo was with her she had to hold herself in reserve, pretend only a mild interest, and it was only when he handed her over to the Balinese liaison officer and they started talking about all the art forms available on the island that her eyes sparkled with enthusiasm and she talked animatedly of the project.

But when Leo came to collect her the eagerness was immediately hidden and she spoke to him with her customary coldness. They were going straight from the site to the tooth-filing ceremony, and all during the drive she sat in silence, trying to work out how she could accept the job and remain unbending in her defiance of Leo without taking that step towards meeting him halfway that he seemed to want so urgently.

Pak Amat and Kartini lived in a village not far from the bungalow, but when they got there it seemed almost a world away from their own Westernised ghetto. Pak Amat came rushing out into the road to welcome them as soon as they arrived, and led them through the *kampung* to his thatched-roofed house, the courtyard of which was gaily decorated with brightly coloured ribbons and flowers, and piled up offerings to the gods: rice, meat, and every variety of fruit. Already the courtyard was crowded with people and Pak Amat introduced them to each one in turn: cousins, uncles, aunts, grandparents, their son's school friends, until Gael's face felt as if it had become fixed in the smile she gave in return to all the friendly greetings. And the names were so confusing; she must have been introduced to as many as ten Ketuts and as many Wayans, at least two of which were in Pak Amat's own family of six children.

When the introductions were at last over they were given seats near a platform spread with a white cloth and Leo said quietly, 'Each child's first name is given according to his order of birth within the family, regardless of whether the child is a boy or girl. The eldest is always Wayan, the second Made, the third Njoman and the fourth Ketut. Then they choose a second name to add on so that the eldest becomes Wayan Sandi or Wayan Donkir or something.'

'But they have six children,' Gael said in a puzzled whisper. 'What do they call the fifth and sixth born?'

Leo grinned. 'When they get to the fifth they start all

over again with Wayan, Made, Njoman and Ketut. Confusing, isn't it? I had a hell of a time employing people at the site until somebody explained the system to me.'

He broke off then as Kartini came into the room proudly leading her son, Ketut Daging, whom she proceeded to wrap in a new white cloth and then he was lifted on to the platform for the ceremony. Gael hadn't known quite what to expect a professional tooth-filer to look like, but he turned out to be quite ordinary, dressed in a white shirt and colourful sarong. First he touched the boy's teeth with a ruby ring and said some words which were guaranteed to stop him from feeling any pain, and admittedly the boy didn't cry out, but his fists were clenched very tight and he looked very pale and scared during the twenty minutes or so it took to turn him from a boy into a man. Gael herself found the process extremely nerve-racking and kept her hands tightly clasped in her lap, looking away as much as she dared without giving offence.

But afterwards she thoroughly enjoyed the feast where everyone sat around eating the dozens of delicious dishes that Kartini had lovingly prepared, chatting and laughing and watching dancers, some as young as five years old, performing traditional dances that were part of their religion, and told old Hindu stories. She had thought that once this was over it would be the end of the ceremony, but it seemed that the highlight of the evening, the *wayang kulit*, or shadowplay, was still to come. The flat cut-out figures were thrown into silhouette by a light behind a large white cloth and the play, one that had been performed for about a thousand years, began—and went on and on. At first Gael tried to follow it, but this was almost impossible when you didn't speak the language. More food and even more of the rice wine was pressed on them at frequent intervals and gradually the alcohol, her sleepless night, and the darkened room, made her begin to nod.

Someone gave her a gentle shake and she woke with a start to find that she had been fast asleep on Leo's shoulder! Hastily she sat up and looked around. The play was over at last and everyone was leaving. They thanked their hosts and Leo helped her into the car. Gael yawned and curled up in the seat.

'I hope they weren't offended that I fell asleep,' she murmured as Leo started the car.

He shook his head. 'They were all too wrapped up in the play to even notice. It's their equivalent of *Gone with the Wind* and they loved every word of it. But we were lucky; that was one of their shorter epics—it only lasted five hours.'

'Five hours? Good heavens! Was I asleep all that time?'

'Most of it.'

Leo stopped the car and Gael sat up, expecting them to be at the bungalow, but he had pulled up on a piece of higher ground where they could look out over the dense equatorial forest to the sea, the wave tips fluorescent in the moonlight.

Leo lit a cigarette and opened the window to let out the smoke. They sat in silence for a while and then he said, 'Have you thought any more about the job I offered you?'

Gael hesitated, then answered honestly, 'I've thought about little else all day, but I—I haven't made up my mind.'

'Anything I can do to help?'

She turned to look at him, sitting so close beside her and yet so very far away, his features thrown into sharp profile from the glow of the cigarette. Taking her courage in both hands, she said, 'Yes, you can tell me the truth. Tell me exactly why you want me to have this job, why your attitude has changed so completely towards me.'

He didn't answer for such a long time that she thought he was going to ignore her question, but then he deliberately stubbed out the cigarette in the ashtray and turned to look at her.

'It's really very simple,' he said slowly. 'You see, I found out that I'm in love with you!'

CHAPTER EIGHT

'What—what did you say?' Gael stared at him, unable to credit her own hearing.

'I said I'm in love with you,' Leo repeated, his voice not quite even. 'I'd stopped wanting to be revenged on you quite some time ago. It wasn't anything sudden, just a gradual process when I saw how unhappy I'd made you, how much I'd hurt you, and began to search my conscience. But finding out that I loved you,' he gave a bitter sort of laugh, 'that happened in about two seconds flat when I saw you standing nearly naked in Dirk Vanderman's arms! I was filled with such uncontrollable jealousy that I wanted to kill him. And if anything was needed to really bring it home to me it was the sick fear I felt when you went crashing down those stairs! The bottom seemed to have dropped out of the world until I got to you and found you were still alive.'

He waited, but when she didn't speak said, 'So there you

have it. That's why I've been trying my damnedest to get through to you, to set our relationship on an even footing in the hope that we can get back together again and start from where we left off in London.' Leaning forward, he reached out and took her slack hand in his. 'I love you, Gael. And I believe you still love me, despite what I've done to you. And I want us to be man and wife, in every sense of the word.'

Her hand trembled violently in his and she couldn't speak, could only stare at him, her eyes made larger by the moonlight. Leo began to draw her towards him, his pulse quickening, but suddenly Gael jerked her hand away and moved as far away from him as possible in the confines of the car.

'How very convenient!' she exclaimed furiously. 'Rumours start spreading that you're a wife-beater and you suddenly find you're head over heels in love with me! You lying hypocrite! Did you really think you had only to say you'd changed your mind and I'd fall willingly into your arms, into your bed? My God, what an egoist you are!'

'Gael, it's true. I wanted to tell you when you were in hospital, but—well, it just didn't seem the right time, so I decided to wait, to try and *show* you that I cared about you.' He sighed. 'Maybe I shouldn't have said anything to you now, but I wanted to be honest with you.'

'Honest? My God, that's funny,' she exclaimed with a bitter laugh. 'Do you really expect me to believe you after the way you deceived me?'

Leo's mouth tightened. 'That's a chance I have to take. If you don't then I have only myself to blame, but it won't be for want of trying. You loved me once. I can only hope that your feelings for me aren't completely dead.'

Gael stared at him in the semi-darkness, wishing that there was more light so that she could see his face clearly, read his expression. Not that that would help, she thought cynically; she had believed he loved her once before and it had all been a sham. At length she broke the silence by saying, 'If you love someone, then you want to make them happy, isn't that right?'

Leo's eyebrows rose. 'It does seem to be the accepted practice,' he agreed.

'And so—if what you say is true and you really love me —you would want to make me happy?'

'Of course.' But his voice sounded wary.

Silkily Gael said, 'Then prove that you love me. Make me happy.'

He turned away and looked through the windscreen, his hands going up to grip the steering wheel. 'By giving you your freedom, I suppose?' he said grimly.

'You suppose correctly. What else would I want from you?' she asked, her voice harsh even to her own ears.

'No.' The word was decisive, unhesitating. 'I'm going to keep you with me just as long as I can.'

Fear sharpened her voice. 'But you promised to let me go after six months!'

His eyes turned to study her anxious face, lit up by a shaft of moonlight, and his voice softened. 'I know, and I'll keep my word. But in the meantime I'm going to do everything in my power to convince you of how much you mean to me.'

Voice heavy with irony, she said, 'You'll be wasting your time. I don't believe a word of it now and I never will.'

Gael took the job with the construction company for the

simple reason that she couldn't resist it, although she told herself that it was because she would go mad if she didn't have something to occupy her. She thoroughly enjoyed travelling round the island to find suitable forms of art-work, the driver of the company car that Leo provided also acting as her interpreter where necessary. At first she had been afraid that it would mean seeing even more of Leo, but after the first few days, when she wasn't touring the island, she did most of the work at the bungalow. And any-way, Leo was completely involved in getting as much work done on the site as possible before the rainy season started, so he often came home much later than he had before and also worked during the weekend sometimes. He was push-ing himself hard and there were lines of tiredness around his eyes, but he still insisted on behaving towards her as if there was nothing between them, talking to her about the project, asking her about her day's travels, taking her out for a meal at one of the big hotels at the weekend. Treating her like a wife, Gael supposed cynically. And it would have been very easy to slip into the role he tried to create for her, to talk animatedly about the colony of obscure wood-carvers she had found, to ask his opinion of a design she had drawn for a wall mural. Once or twice she had even caught herself doing exactly that and had stopped short, her eyes full of unspoken hatred as she glared at him. And for a while then the tension between them had become solid and tangible until Leo had again deliberately set out to break it down.

The weather became sultry and extremely humid, the ground arid and parched after the long dry season. The rains were late in coming that year and tempers became frayed as everyone waited for the weather to break. When

they did at last arrive they came unexpectedly in the middle
of the night, came with a jagged flash of lightning and the
great, rolling thunderclaps of an electric storm, the first of
which shook the bungalow as if an earthquake had hit it.

Gael sat up in bed with a startled scream, not knowing
what was happening. Lightning blinded her eyes and another rolling burst of thunder almost overhead made her
put her hands tightly over her ears. So she didn't see or hear
Leo when he came into her room, was only aware of his
presence when he sat down on her bed and put his arms
round her.

'There's nothing to be afraid of. It's only a storm.' He
had to shout in her ear, the thunder was so deafening.

She nodded. 'I'm all right. It just startled me.'

But he didn't let her go. His eyes grew dark with desire
as the lightning showed him her hair falling loose and
tousled about her shoulders, the soft outline of her breasts
under the thin, low-cut nightdress.

'Gael.' He breathed her name as his arms tightened
around her.

'No! No, Leo, please!'

But already his mouth had found hers, his lips hard and
demanding, fired by a fierce hunger that brooked no denial.
She tried to fight him, to bite his lip, to claw at his face, but
he caught her wrists and bore her back against the pillow,
using his weight to hold her down while he continued to
ravage her mouth compulsively. Then suddenly she wasn't
fighting him any more, her mouth moved under his but
only to return his kiss, lost in the fierceness of his embrace.
She was aware of nothing but his mouth on hers, of his
hands that had let go of her wrists and had begun to explore
her body. Seemingly of their own volition her arms slid

round his neck and she moaned as he bared her shoulder and kissed her neck, her throat. Thunder reverberated around the room as he drew the nightdress further down and his lips, soft and sensuous now, found her breast. She gave a gasping cry of ecstasy and her fingers fastened in his hair as her body arched beneath him.

'Gael! Oh, my darling girl, I want you so much.' He was throwing off his robe, pushing the covers aside, climbing into bed with her. Lightning lit his face, dark and intent, as he again reached out for her.

'No!' Throwing herself out of bed, Gael ran towards the window, banging herself on the furniture and almost falling over in her frantic scramble to get away from him.

'Gael——' Leo started to come after her, but she screamed hysterically.

'Don't touch me! Oh, God, leave me alone, leave me alone!' She stood against the wall, quivering with emotion, her trembling fingers trying to pull up her nightdress and cover herself.

Slowly Leo stood up and shrugged himself into his robe, taking his time about it. Then he said heavily, 'All right, I'll leave you alone—tonight. But some time we're going to make love. It's going to happen between us. You know it is—because you want it as much as I do.' He turned as another great clap of sound shook the house and walked out of the room.

From that moment on the atmosphere between them was like a detonator, just waiting for a spark to make it erupt into an explosion of fire and passion. Gael could only try to preserve an icy indifference and to keep as far away from Leo as possible, cursing herself a hundred times a day for letting her stupid body take over from her head, even if only for such a few brief moments.

Only once did they speak of it and that was when she flinched away when Leo went to help her into the car and he said scathingly, 'Afraid that if I touch you you'll show your real feelings again, Gael?'

'Feelings didn't come into it,' she replied shortly. 'It was only sex.'

'*Only* sex?'

'Yes.' Fiercely she said, 'I don't want to talk about it. I was frightened by the storm and didn't—didn't realise what was happening.'

His eyes mocked her but he said nothing, just started the car and drove away, but Gael had the uneasy feeling that she hadn't convinced him at all.

Everyone breathed a sigh of relief when the thunderstorm came, it proved to be only a false break in the weather, bringing little rain. And after it the air became even more sultry, so that it was an effort to move outside the air-conditioned coolness of the bungalow. Even the native Balinese felt it, and Leo reported that the foremen were having difficulty controlling the labour force at the hospital site, added to which there was trouble between the Indonesians and the migrant population of Chinese workers, who—although nearly all of them were second generation and had been born in Bali—had never been integrated into the community and were greatly resented when there was so little work to be shared among so many people.

Although Leo made light of it, Gael was aware of the increasing unrest from what she observed in her travels round the island. Most of the tourists had left now and so there were more people out of work, and she noticed an air of anxiety among some of the people she had to deal with, so it came as no great surprise when Leo told her to call a halt to her trips for a while.

'It will be better when the rains come, but in the meantime you'd better concentrate on your designs and things. You can do that here, can't you?'

'Yes, of course. But can't I even come up to the site?'

'Better not,' Leo said emphatically. 'If you need anything I'll bring it for you. And you'd better tell Pak Amat to lay in a store of groceries, just in case supplies get difficult.'

Gael's eyes widened in surprise. 'Is it really as bad as that?'

He shrugged. 'I don't know. It may not be. But Indonesia has had a troubled history in recent years and the political situation is by no means stable. What may start as a small incident could always grow into a major confrontation. And I intend to take as many precautions as possible.' He looked at her frowningly. 'You'll probably be safe enough on the estate or on the beach, but don't get any ideas about going off further afield on your own. Okay?'

Gael nodded. 'Yes, all right.'

Pak Amat and Kartini, too, were obviously worried about the situation, although they turned up for work every day as usual, but it took them much longer on their shopping trips and often they couldn't get as much as they had hoped, dairy goods especially being almost impossible to obtain. Gael did as Leo had asked and restricted herself to the immediate area, but the weather was so oppressive that she seldom went further than the beach.

Then one day the two Balinese servants didn't turn up.

'I don't like leaving you here alone,' Leo said worriedly. 'Perhaps it would be better if you went to stay with one of the other wives.'

'I'm perfectly all right,' Gael answered firmly. 'They're

probably just late. But if they don't turn up I'll go and spend the day with Moira Stanton or somebody, if it will make you any happier.'

'It will—considerably.' He hesitated a moment, his eyes searching her face, then he reached out to take her hand. 'Gael, I . . .'

Immediately she snatched it back, her mouth set and hard. 'Why don't you go, there's nothing for you here!' she reminded him sharply.

A bleak, fed-up look came into his eyes before he turned on his heel and strode to the car.

Gael tried to concentrate on her work, but found it difficult to settle. At noon, when the servants still hadn't arrived, she made herself a salad and then walked round to Tom and Moira Stanton's house, but found the place deserted, securely locked and with shutters over the windows. For a moment she stood nonplussed; the nearest people she knew were Malcolm and Norah Taylor, but her mind shrank from going there since the woman's insinuations about Leo; she could just imagine the prodding questions about her personal life that would be aimed at her. And right now her private life with Leo was in no state to stand any kind of probing.

She decided to go back to her own bungalow and hurried towards it, but halfway there she heard a loud explosion and saw a cloud of black smoke going up into the air from the direction of the hospital site a mile or so away. This was followed by a lot of sharper, popping noises that sounded horribly like the noise of gunfire that she'd heard on TV newsreels back home. Gael broke into a run and didn't stop until she was safely back in the bungalow, dripping with perspiration, her clothes clinging to her. Immediately she grabbed the phone to call Leo, to find out what had happened. But the line was completely dead. She jabbed at it uselessly for a few minutes, then flung the receiver down with a sob. She had to know what had happened—she had to! Running outside to the shed, she caught hold of her bicycle and dragged it out. Oh, no! She hadn't used it for so long that the tire was flat. With fumbling fingers she undid the pump and bent to blow it up.

'*Njonya?*'

A hand touched her arm and Gael shrieked with fright.

'*Njonya*, do not be afraid. It is Kartini.'

A sob of relief escaped Gael as she recognised the native woman's features in the dim light of the shed. 'I'm sorry, you startled me.' She became aware of the woman's tight grip on her arm, of the tension in her bearing. 'What is it, Kartini? Is Pak Amat with you?'

'No, he sent me to find Tuan Kane, to ask him to help us. Please, where is the Tuan?'

'He isn't here, Kartini, he's at the hospital site.' Gael remembered again the explosion and a shudder of fear ran through her. But then she saw that Kartini was weeping and reluctantly put down the pump. 'You'd better come inside and tell me what's the matter.'

She took the native woman inside and sat her in a chair with a glass of brandy and water. 'It is our son, Ketut Darging,' Kartini told her when her weeping had steadied a little. 'There has been fighting among the students and he has been hurt. I fear that the gods will claim him,' she added on a fresh burst of weeping. 'He bleeds so much. None of our medicines will stop it, so Pak Amat sent me for Tuan Kane. He said Tuan Kane will know what to do.'

Gael gazed at her in horror. 'But don't you have a doctor in your village?'

Kartini shook her hed. 'The nearest is very far away and must go to the army hospital if there is any trouble. And— and,' she sought for the English words, 'if we tell that Ketut has been hurt in a fight he may be punished.' She look up at Gael hopelessly, tears pouring down her face.

Gael looked at her grimly, wondering how on earth she could help, her fears about the explosion at the construction site of necessity pushed to the back of her mind. Realising that there was only one thing to be done, she once again tried to phone in the vain hope that it might be working, but it was still dead.

Firmly she took the elder woman's arm and helped her to her feet. 'Come on, we'll go to the hospital and find Dr Stanton. He'll be able to help you.'

Kartini had come on her bicycle and when Gael had finished pumping up her tire the two set out for the hospital. Only then did Gael realise how dark the day had become. Great black clouds hung low in the sky and a fresh breeze was starting to blow in from the sea. They reached the hospital without incident and Gael hurried to find the doctor. She had to wait for some time because he was attending to a patient, and when she explained the situation he refused point-blank to go with her.

'No, I can't leave here. Heaven knows how many patients may be brought in before the night's out, and probably in a far worse condition than your servant's boy.'

He went to hurry away, but Gael caught his arm. 'But what am I going to do?' she said desperately. 'We can't just let him die!'

A harassed look came into Tom's eyes; the possibility of having his hospital turned into a clearing station for wounded men was a far cry from the gently-paced practice he was used to. 'All I can do is to arrange to let you have a car and a driver to collect the boy and bring him here.'

'All right. Thank you.' He went to walk away to see to it, but Gael stopped him. 'Please, is there any news from the construction site? I heard an explosion.'

He shook his head, worry in his eyes. 'No, nothing, yet.'

Gael didn't attempt to detain him further and before long she and Kartini were sitting in the back of a big saloon car as the native driver drove fast towards Kartini's village. Before they had gone a mile the heavens opened and the torrential rain turned the dry, dusty road into a slippery stream of mud. The car of necessity slowed, the driver hardly able to see out of the windscreen although the wipers were going flat out to try to clear it. Once Kartini didn't call out a turning in time and they had to turn, the wheels gouging great ruts in the mud before the wheels bit into solid ground and they pulled free of the morass at last.

They were more than halfway there before the first hint of trouble came. Came hidden by the noise of the storm until a bullet smashed and screeched its way along the metalwork of the roof, quickly followed by another that shattered a side window but missed them completely. The driver gave a scream of fright and put his foot down hard on the accelerator, the car bucketing wildly along the road, swerving from side to side as the man fought to see where he was going in the driving rain. The car suddenly lurched and came to a violent standstill. Gael lost her hold on the door handle and fell heavily against the side of the car, Kartini on top of her.

Whimpering with fear, the driver feverishly started the engine again, screaming the accelerator in an attempt to get free of the mud that held them. 'Is no good. It won't move!' he shouted despairingly.

'I'll try to push.' Gael got out of the car and was immediately soaked to the skin, but surprisingly the rain was quite warm. The car was swerved sideways across the road, its back wheels embedded in the mud, and Gael had to literally wade through the running water to reach it. She was sure as much rain had come down already as would have lasted Manchester for a year!

Kartini came to help her while the driver revved the engine, but all that happened was that the two women were covered in mud that sprayed up from the spinning tires. Then the sound of another shot carried clearly to their ears. The driver leapt out of the car, his face petrified.

'We must leave the car. We must go back!'

'But we have to get to the village. A boy could be dying!'

But even before she had finished speaking the man had run into the thick forest and left them alone.

Grimly Gael turned off the engine and the lights, then set to work to gather stones and branches to set under the back wheels. It took ages, and there was always the constant fear that some marauding gang would come upon them, so she made Kartini keep a look-out while she worked, ready at the first shout of warning to drop everything and take to the forest. It took almost an hour before they broke free of the mud, an hour that seemed like a year, but no one came near them and they heard no more sounds of gunfire.

The *kampung* seemed to be deserted when Gael drove into it and switched off the engine, but most of the people were in Pak Amat's house, crowding round the boy and giv-

ing advice so that the atmosphere in the room was hot and
foetid.

Pak Amat rushed forward as soon as he saw Kartini, his
face breaking into dismay when he didn't see Leo. But
then Kartini broke into voluble explanations and he
caught Gael's hand and wrung it, tears of gratitude in his
eyes. They gave her some rice wine to drink while the boy
was being wrapped up and some prayers said over him by
the local priest, and Kartini found her some dry clothes; a
sarong and a loose *kebaya* or blouse, held in place by a
length of cloth tied round her waist. They held umbrellas
over them while they got the boy in the car, Kartini sitting
in the back with him, and Pak Amat beside Gael to show
her the way.

Then the car wouldn't start! Gael tried the engine until
she was afraid of running the battery flat. She asked Pak
Amat if there was any one in the village who knew about
engines, but he shook his head helplessly. She swore under
her breath and got out of the car to lift up the hood. In two
seconds the new clothes were as wet as the ones she had
taken off. The torrential rain had got into the engine while
it had been standing and the plugs were soaking wet.
Cursing herself for not having thought of the possibility,
Gael took the plugs out and dried them off as best she
could, thanking her stars that she had taken a course in car
maintenance at evening classes, although the likelihood of
having to repair a car in a monsoon and with a native
uprising going on around her hadn't exactly been on her
mind at the time, she thought with mocking self-irony. Pak
Amat brought a piece of tarpaulin, which they tied across
the hood to keep the rain out and then tried the engine
again. Still the darn thing wouldn't start.

'You'll have to give me a push!' she yelled through the window.

All the men came willingly enough and Gael held her breath as they picked up speed and she let out the clutch. The car bucked and jerked and for a minute she didn't think they were going to make it, but then the blessed thing coughed into life and she pressed down the accelerator to make sure it stayed that way. While she had been fixing the car the sun had set, although the sky had been so dark that she had hardly noticed it, but now the pitch blackness of the night made the going that much more difficult and the hours of rain had made the road far more treacherous, the surface washed away completely in some parts. Where the road was bordered by trees it wasn't so bad because it was easy to see where it went, but in the open country it was almost impossible to tell which was the road at all at times. If it hadn't been for Pak Amat's knowledge of the country-side Gael was sure she would have become hopelessly lost long ago, but even with his help she missed the road at times and twice got bogged down in the soft verges and had to get out and cut down tree branches with Pak Amat's knife to give a solid purchase. Gael grew increasingly anxious about the boy, but it was impossible to go any faster.

She did, however, put her foot down when they came to the place where they had been shot at on the way in. Gripping the wheel tightly, she headed down the gap in the trees lit up by the tunnelling beam of the headlights, ready to duck at the sound of a shot. Not that that would do any good; she remembered reading somewhere that a bullet travelled faster than sound; you would be dead before you even heard it. The ghoulish thought made her go even faster, but then they rounded a bend and she slammed her

brakes on with all the strength in her legs. The car skidded
and travelled sideways down the road and came to a halt
only a couple of feet away from a tree that lay squarely
across the entire road with no passage at either side.

'Get down!' Gael flung herself sideways, expecting a
fusillade of bullets to come tearing into the car from the
men who had felled the tree to form an ambush. Pak Amat
threw himself down beside her, his eyes rolling in fear,
while Kartini in the back made little sobbing noises and
the boy moaned in delirium.

Gael could feel the hairs on the back of her neck standing up in fright as she waited for what seemed an eternity,
but no shots came, no shouts of triumph, nothing. Slowly
she lifted her head and looked out, terrified at what she
might see, but there was no one there ready to drag her out
into the wildness of the night. But there was no knowing
when they might come back. Hastily she restarted the car,
afraid that it might get wet and stall again if she didn't
keep it running, then she straightened it up and went to
look at the tree. A quick examination showed her that the
roots had been washed out of the ground by the rain and
the tree had been felled by its own weight. It wasn't very
big, but it had a lot of branches that they would have to cut
through if they were to get by.

Pak Amat set to work at once and Gael found a tire lever
in the trunk that she used to hack at some of the smaller
branches. They had been working doggedly for nearly half
an hour when Gael thought she heard an alien noise
through the drumming of the rain. She touched Pak Amat
on the arm. 'Listen!'

He put his head on one side and then they both heard
the noise and recognised it. It was the noise of a car being

driven fast along the road towards them! For a moment blind panic gripped her. What if it was the rebels coming back?

'We must hide! Quickly!'

They ran back to the car and took the boy from Kartini, Pak Amat and Gael carrying him between them. He was only semi-conscious now, delirious from fever and loss of blood. They handled him as gently as they could, but even so he groaned aloud as they hurried deeper into the trees. But the car came before they could get very far and they had to crouch down among the many trunks of a giant banyan tree, a tree that sent feelers down from its upper branches which took root in the ground and eventually became secondary trunks.

The car came to a stop on the other side of the fallen tree, its headlights piercing the darkness. Gael heard the door slam as someone got out and she could imagine them climbing over the branches of the tree to examine their car, and even though she had taken the precaution of switching off the engine and the lights, it would need only a touch to feel that the engine was still warm. Then they would find where they had been trying to cut away the tree, and the blood on the back seat would tell them that someone was wounded. The men would come to look for them then, knowing that they couldn't possibly have gone far. Gael bit hard into her hand to stop herself from sobbing aloud. They didn't stand a chance!

They could hear someone coming now, quietly pushing their way through the dense undergrowth. Pak Amat stood up, his knife gripped in his hand in the stabbing position. Gael's eyes widened in horror, but she, too, picked up a log of wood and straightened up, ready to fight. The noise came nearer now. Impossible to tell how many. The bushes only a few yards away were pushed gently aside and a man's dark figure moved to go past without seeing them. Gael began to breathe again, but then behind them the boy moaned and a flashlight suddenly split the darkness, shining right on them! Pak Amat braced himself to run forward, but then a voice she recognised gave a great shout.

'Gael!'

'Leo! It's Leo!'

She dropped the piece of wood and ran towards him. Leo caught her in his arms and crushed her to him, held her tight—so tight.

'Thank God I found you! I've been half out of my mind!'

'Oh, Leo, I'm so glad you've come! I was so afraid'.

They both began to speak at once, Gael clinging to him in a relief that was overwhelming. But then he cut her short by kissing her hard on the mouth, regardless of the monsoon and the danger, regardless of everything but the knowledge that she was safe and in his arms.

He raised his head, his eyes glinting into hers, then seemed to come back to reality. 'There was blood in that car, have you got Pak Amat's boy?'

'Yes, he's here. We were trying to cut through the tree.'

'We'll take him in my car. Here, hold this.' Leo thrust the flashlight into her hands and strode to where Kartini still crouched beneath the banyan. He lifted the boy into his arms easily and Gael guided him back to the road. Leo took charge of the situation at once and soon they were headed in the direction of the hospital again.

It was strange; the conditions were just as bad, the danger from the rioters was still there, but now she felt

completely safe, had handed over her responsibilities to
Leo without a thought, confident that he would get them
through. Only once were they in any danger; as they
passed through the outskirts of a village they disturbed a
band of men who were looting a shop and the looters ran at
them, trying to bar their passage, but Leo simply put his
foot on the accelerator, his hand on the horn, and drove
through them, the men leaping out of the way.

At the hospital Tom Stanton took over their patient and
Pak Amat and Kartini thanked them volubly before hurrying after him.

Leo looked at Gael. 'And now, young lady, I think I'd
better take you home so you can get dry. You must be
frozen in those wet clothes!'

'A hot shower would be nice,' Gael admitted. 'But
you're soaked too,' she added, seeing how his shirt clung to
him, outlining his broad chest and muscular shoulders.

'I'll live.'

'How did you know where to find us?' Gael asked as he
began to drive towards the bungalow.

'The army took over at the hospital site when the rioters
blew up the gas store and so there wasn't any need for me
to stay there.'

'Was that the explosion I heard?' Gael broke in.

'Probably. It went up with a hell of a bang. But I think it
frightened the rioters more than it did us, because the
army had no difficulty in rounding them up. It wasn't
much of a riot, really, more an outburst of tension because
the rains were late, and it should all have died out by the
morning. Where was I? Oh, yes. I naturally hurried home
to make sure you were all right and found the place empty,
the doors unlocked and your bike gone. I thought perhaps

you'd panicked and gone to stay with someone.'

'So you went to Tom Stanton?'

His voice changed. 'No, not at first. I thought that perhaps you'd gone to Dirk Vanderman, so I went to his place.'

'Oh.' Gael could think of nothing else to say.

'You weren't there, of course, and I stayed only long enough for him to ram a few home truths down by throat. Oh, and he gave me that.'

He indicated a piece of rolled-up paper tucked into the parcel shelf. Wonderingly Gael took it out and unrolled it. It was the painting of Leo that she had done from memory. 'Oh,' she said again, equally inadequately.

'That, of course, made me even more determined than ever to find you and I went to Tom Stanton's place and then on to the hospital.' Dryly he added, 'I expect you can imagine just what I had to say to him when I found he'd let you go off into the danger zone with only a driver to protect you. Although Tom did say that he hadn't expected you to go along as well and ran out to stop you when he saw you driving off, but was too late. What happened to the driver, by the way?'

'Oh, he ran away when the bullets hit us. Oh dear, I suppose I ought to have looked for him on the way back.'

'Bullets!' The car swerved as Leo took his eyes off the road, but he swiftly righted it again.

'It's all right,' Gael assured him. 'They were unlucky, they only hit the car, not us.'

'That isn't *quite* how I would have described it,' said Leo, his voice sharp with anger.

'No. Well, it's all over now. We're both safe.'

Leo pulled into the driveway of the bungalow and switched off the engine and the lights. He turned to look at her, the rain drumming loudly on the roof of the car. 'Yes,' he said softly. 'I think we're both home safely now. Aren't we?'

'Yes. Oh, yes!' Gael gazed at him for a long moment, the love that had never really died shining in her eyes again, then she reached to pull his head down to hers, to kiss him with all the pent-up hunger that she had been holding back for so long.

It was a long time before they drew apart. Leo gently lifted a finger to wipe the tears of happiness from her eyes. Then he grinned. 'If you still want proof that I love you, you only have to look in the mirror. You look terrible!'

Gael laughed. 'You don't exactly look like a Greek god yourself right now!'

They sprinted from the car to the bungalow, to stand dripping in the hallway.

'I've a feeling you're going to insist on having the bathroom first,' Leo remarked, his eyes warm as he looked at her.

'I certainly am!'

'Tut tut!' He shook his head resignedly. 'Whatever happened to Women's Lib?'

It was wonderful to strip off her filthy clothes and to step under the hot shower, feel the water cleaning the mud from her hair and body. Gael closed her eyes and began to soap herself, her heart singing with happiness, because she knew that everything was going to be all right. His face when he had seen her in the jungle had told her more plainly than words ever could just how much Leo cared.

She gave a sudden gasp as she realised that another pair of hands had begun to soap her, sinuously caressing the curves of her body. Her pulse started to race and she trembled violently, stiffening under his touch. But Leo deliberately pulled her back against him until his hard body was supporting hers, his hands exploring, creating waves of sensuality that made her moan with desire. Only when she relaxed against him, gave way to the sensations he aroused in her, did he turn her round to face him and take her mouth, kissing her with a passion that sent the room whirling around her. Then he turned off the shower and put on his bathrobe while he wrapped her in a big thick towel and dried her hair, taking delight in seeing the strands restored to their golden colour. When it was dry he picked her up and carried her into the bedroom.

They hadn't spoken much, there had been no need for words, but as he laid her gently on the bed and went to remove her towel, Gael put out a hand to stop him.

'Leo, there's something I have to tell you.'

He became very still. 'That's a classic-sounding line. If it's about Dirk Vanderman ...'

'No. No, it isn't about Dirk,' Gael said gently. 'He wasn't my lover. In fact,' she flushed, 'I've never had a lover.' His hand tightened convulsively on hers, but before he could speak she went on quickly, 'It's about the accident when your girl-friend was killed.'

'It doesn't matter,' Leo broke in fiercely. 'Not any more.'

'But it does to me. Please, Leo, let me finish. I told you the truth when I said I wasn't responsible. I wasn't even driving the car that night. It was my brother-in-law, Clive. He was afraid that if he lost his licence it would cost him his job and so I agreed to take the blame.'

Leo stared down at her. 'Then all this time ... Why didn't you tell me?'

Gael's hand turned to cover his. 'I tried to at first, but

you wouldn't listen, and afterwards I knew you'd never believe me.'

'Dear God, no wonder you hated me so much! Oh, Gael, my little love, how can you possibly forgive me?'

She smiled at him tenderly. 'Easily. If you hadn't been so all fired up to get your revenge we might never have met, might never have had—this.'

He bent to kiss her gently and then looked at her quizzically. 'You're quite sure you have nothing else to tell me?'

Gael lay back on the pillows and looked up into his face, so dear, so beloved. She remembered the man who had been killed in the car with his fiancée, but she would never tell him about that. Let him hold the memory of her in his heart if he wanted to. Gael was alive and knew that she had all his love now.

'Quite sure,' she said firmly, and opened her arms to take him to her.

HARLEQUIN SUPERROMANCE

LOVE'S EMERALD FLAME
WILLA LAMBERT

A Contemporary Love Story

The steaming jungle of Peru was the stage
for their love. Diana Green, a spirited
and beautiful young journalist, who became
a willing pawn in a dangerous game...
and Sloane Hendriks, a lonely desperate
man, driven by a secret he would
reveal to no one.

Love's Emerald Flame is the second stunning novel in
this timely new series of modern love stories—
HARLEQUIN SUPERROMANCES.

Longer, exciting, sensual and dramatic, these
compelling new books are for you—the woman of today!

Watch for HARLEQUIN SUPERROMANCE #2, Love's Emerald
Flame, in November wherever paperback books are sold
or order your copy from

Harlequin Reader Service

In U.S.A.
MPO Box 707
Niagara Falls, NY 14302

In Canada
649 Ontario St.
Stratford, Ont. N5A 6W2

SPECIAL

Harlequin Romance Treasury Book Offer

This superb Romance Treasury is yours at little or <u>no</u> cost.

3 exciting, full-length Romance novels in one beautiful hard-cover book.

**Introduce yourself to
Harlequin Romance Treasury.
The most beautiful books you've ever seen!**

Cover and spine of each volume features a distinctive gilt design.
An elegant bound-in ribbon bookmark completes the classic design.
No detail has been overlooked to make Romance Treasury
volumes as beautiful and lasting as the stories they contain.
What a delightful way to enjoy the very best and most popular
Harlequin romances again and again!

Here's how to get your volume NOW!

MAIL IN	$	GET
2 SPECIAL PROOF-OF-PURCHASE SEALS*	PLUS $1 U.S.	ONE BOOK
5 SPECIAL PROOF-OF-PURCHASE SEALS*	PLUS 50¢ U.S.	ONE BOOK
8 SPECIAL PROOF-OF-PURCHASE SEALS*	FREE	ONE BOOK

*Special proof-of-purchase seal from inside back cover of all specially marked Harlequin "Let Your Imagination Fly Sweepstakes" volumes. No other proof-of-purchase accepted.

ORDERING DETAILS:

Print your name, address, city, state or province, zip or postal code on the coupon below or a plain 3" x 5" piece of paper and together with the special proof-of-purchase seals and check or money order (no stamps or cash please) as indicated. Mail to:

HARLEQUIN ROMANCE TREASURY BOOK OFFER P.O. BOX 1399 MEDFORD, N.Y. 11763, U.S.A.

Make check or money order payable to: Harlequin Romance Treasury Offer. Allow 3 to 4 weeks for delivery.

Special offer expires: June 30, 1981

PLEASE PRINT

Name

Address

Apt. No.

City

State/ Prov.

Zip/Postal Code

Let Your Imagination Fly Sweepstakes

Rules and Regulations:

NO PURCHASE NECESSARY

1. Enter the Let Your Imagination Fly Sweepstakes 1, 2 or 3 as often as you wish. Mail each entry form separately bearing sufficient postage. Specify the sweepstake you wish to enter on the outside of the envelope. Mail a completed entry form or, your name, address, and telephone number printed on a plain 3" x 5" piece of paper to:
HARLEQUIN LET YOUR IMAGINATION FLY SWEEPSTAKES,
P.O. BOX 1280, MEDFORD, N.Y. 11763 U.S.A.

2. Each completed entry form must be accompanied by 1 Let Your Imagination Fly proof-of-purchase seal from the back inside cover of specially marked Let Your Imagination Fly Harlequin books (or the words "Let Your Imagination Fly" printed on a plain 3" x 5" piece of paper. Specify by number the Sweepstakes you are entering on the outside of the envelope.

3. The prize structure for each sweepstake is as follows:

Sweepstake 1 - North America

Grand Prize winner's choice: a one-week trip for two to either Bermuda; Montreal, Canada; or San Francisco. 3 Grand Prizes will be awarded (min. approx. retail value $1,375. U.S., based on Chicago departure) and 4,000 First Prizes: scarves by nik nik, worth $14. U.S. each. All prizes will be awarded.

Sweepstake 2 - Caribbean

Grand Prize winner's choice: a one-week trip for two to either Nassau, Bahamas; San Juan, Puerto Rico; or St. Thomas, Virgin Islands. 3 Grand Prizes will be awarded. (Min. approx. retail value $1,650. U.S., based on Chicago departure) and 4,000 First Prizes: simulated diamond pendants by Kenneth Jay Lane, worth $15. U.S. each. All prizes will be awarded.

Sweepstake 3 - Europe

Grand Prize winner's choice: a one-week trip for two to either London, England; Frankfurt, Germany; Paris, France; or Rome, Italy. 3 Grand Prizes will be awarded. (Min. approx. retail value $2,800. U.S., based on Chicago departure) and 4,000 First Prizes: 1/2 oz. bottles of perfume, BLAZER by Anne Klein. (Retail value over $30. U.S.). All prizes will be awarded.

Grand trip prizes will include coach round-trip airfare for two persons from the nearest commercial airport serviced by Delta Air Lines to the city as designated in the prize, double occupancy accommodation at a first-class or medium hotel, depending on vacation, and $500. U.S. spending money. Departure taxes, visas, passports, ground transportation to and from airports will be the responsibility of the winners.

4. To be eligible, Sweepstakes entries must be received as follows:
Sweepstake 1 Entries received by February 28, 1981
Sweepstake 2 Entries received by April 30, 1981
Sweepstake 3 Entries received by June 30, 1981
Make sure you enter each Sweepstake separately since entries will not be carried forward from one Sweepstake to the next.

The odds of winning will be determined by the number of entries received in each of the three sweepstakes. Canadian residents, in order to win any prize, will be required to first correctly answer a time-limited skill-testing question, to be posed by telephone, at a mutually convenient time.

5. Random selections to determine Sweepstake 1, 2 or 3 winners will be conducted by Lee Krost Associates, an independent judging organization whose decisions are final. Only one prize per family, per sweepstake. Prizes are non-transferable and non-refundable and no substitutions will be allowed. Winners will be responsible for any applicable federal, state and local taxes. Trips must be taken during normal tour periods before June 30, 1982. Reservations will be on a space-available basis. Airline tickets are non-transferable, non-refundable and non-redeemable for cash.

6. The Let Your Imagination Fly Sweepstakes is open to all residents of the United States of America and Canada, (excluding the Province of Quebec) except employees and their immediate families of Harlequin Enterprises Ltd., its advertising agencies, Marketing & Promotion Group Canada Ltd. and Lee Krost Associates, Inc., the independent judging company. Winners may be required to furnish proof of eligibility. Void wherever prohibited or restricted by law. All federal, state, provincial and local laws apply.

7. For a list of trip winners, send a stamped, self-addressed envelope to:
Harlequin Trip Winners List, P.O. Box 1401, MEDFORD, N.Y. 11763 U.S.A.
Winners lists will be available after the last sweepstake has been conducted and winners determined.
NO PURCHASE NECESSARY.

Let Your Imagination Fly Sweepstakes

OFFICIAL ENTRY FORM

Please enter me in Sweepstake No. _____

Please print:
Name

Address

Apt. No.   City

State/   Zip/Postal
Prov.   Code

Telephone No.   area code
( )

MAIL TO:
HARLEQUIN LET YOUR
IMAGINATION FLY SWEEPSTAKE No. ___
P.O. BOX 1280,
MEDFORD, N.Y. 11763 U.S.A.
(Please specify by number, the Sweepstake you are entering.)